THERE'S NO PLACE LIKE
HOME
AT CHRISTMAS

COLLECTED BY
SHANE LENNON

EDITED BY
JONATHAN IRWIN

MERCIER PRESS
IRISH PUBLISHER – IRISH STORY

MERCIER PRESS

Cork

www.mercierpress.ie

© Individual contributors, 2010

ISBN: 978 1 85635 710 4

10 9 8 7 6 5 4 3 2 1

A CIP record for this title is available from the British Library

Printed and bound in the EU.

CONTENTS

FOREWORD

There really is no place like home, especially at Christmas time. For me, it's still the most unbelievably magical time of year: steeped in traditions and rituals, with friends dropping by, family flocking home, shopping lists to tick off – without ticking off each other – trees to decorate, presents to wrap, a feast to prepare … Most importantly though, it's a time to count our blessings, pull our loved ones closer and bask in the glow of friendship and hope.

Christmas is a particularly challenging time for the families we support through the Jack & Jill Foundation: families with very sick children to be nursed and loved in their home – in the middle of all this magic and mayhem All year round we endeavour to give our families the gift of time – time to do those normal things that others take for granted like sleeping, shopping and getting on with life, with the peace of mind that their sick child is being well cared for. Never is our support in more demand,

more important and more appreciated than at Christmas. By supporting this book you are supporting our service. Thank you.

I must admit that when Shane Lennon and the team from Dundalk IT came to us with their idea for a children's book of short stories, we were both excited and daunted by the prospect. Would it work? Would the right authors sign up? Would the stories arrive? Would Mercier jump on board? Would it be ready on time and would it sell? The one thing we were certain about was the title and it just had to be *There's No Place Like Home* – because that's the very essence of Jack & Jill.

We needn't have worried and we are delighted with the book and confident that it will fly. It has Christmas magic by the bucketful and I want to thank all the authors for that. All busy people, in high demand, and all ready, willing and very able to pen a special story for Jack & Jill. Thank you.

Choosing this book is like giving our families a gentle push up the hill. Thank you for that helping hand and enjoy the read, the magic and the view from the top.

Jonathan Irwin

CEO & Founder of Jack & Jill Children's Foundation
www.jackandjill.ie

❄ 💜 ❄

THE SMALLEST ELF

CIARA GERAGHTY
(with much assistance from Neil MacLochlainn, aged 9)

You know the way grown-ups always ask you what you want
to be when you grow up? Well, I never had any problem
answering that question. Because I always knew. I never
had any doubts. I wanted to work for Father Christmas.
In the workshop. You know the one. Where the Christmas
toys are made. Even before I did my Elementary Elf exams
(I passed them all!), Mama says that I did nothing but talk
about being one of Santa's elves. She says I dressed up like
them, using green leaves that I found in the fairy fort at the
bottom of our garden. Making pointed hats out of green
crêpe paper and sticking blocks of wood onto the heels
of my shoes, the way elves do to make themselves seem a
little taller. Because you see, elves are small. Tiny in fact.

And that suits me down to the ground. Because I am tiny too.

But there's a difference between pretending to be something and actually being that very thing. Because now I am one of Santa's elves. The trouble is, I'm not a very good one. In the first place, I'm the smallest elf in the workshop. I have to stand on an upside-down bucket to reach my workbench and even then my eyes can just about see over the edge. And I'm not just small.

'Butterfingers,' Flint calls me when I drop a fire engine – a toy one – on his toe.

'Slowcoach,' Copper might say when I'm the last to get a needle threaded.

Butch – the tallest elf – just calls me Tiny and even though I am tiny, it doesn't sound great. Not the way he says it.

When things go wrong at the workshop it's usually my fault. Take the other day for instance. I was working at the Laughometre. I suppose you're wondering what a Laughometre does? So did I when I first arrived. Well, it's probably the biggest machine in the workshop, all blinking lights and switches and knobs and buttons. Anytime a child laughs – and I mean any child, anywhere in the world – this laugh, or giggle, or chortle or chuckle or even gurgle, gets sent to the Laughometre. Don't ask me how. And these laughs, and giggles, chortles, chuckles and even gurgles, are whipped like cream into the sort of energy that we need to make all the other machines in the workshop – like the snow-dome and the windmill and the paper-shaker – work.

Anyway, I checked the screen to see what kind of laugh was coming in and I could have sworn it was a chortle so I pulled on the chortle lever. I have to jump on it and hold on tight to pull it down enough to get the chortle into the machine. It's hard work, believe me. But it wasn't a chortle after all. It was a chuckle. And Miss Pritchett – who is in charge of the workshop – never gets tired of telling me how important it is not to mix up any of the laughs. The chortles have to go with the chortles and the chuckles with the chuckles. Otherwise, the system gets clogged up, she says. And boy did the system get clogged up that day. A lot of laughs leaked out of the machine and that slowed all the other machines and made the workshop sound like a very funny place, what with all the giggles and chortles and chuckles and gurgles lying in puddles all over the floor. But it wasn't one bit funny. I was put on fairy-dust duty afterwards, which is the easiest job in the place. Everybody knows that.

You're probably wondering what we use the fairy dust for? Well, I happen to know the answer to that one. It's what Father Christmas sprinkles in the eyes of any child who happens to see him on Christmas Eve. Some children hide behind the curtains in their sitting-rooms you know. Or under their beds. Last year, one little boy hid in the coal bucket beside the fire place. But if you're planning on doing that next Christmas Eve, take my advice and don't bother. Because once the fairy dust gets sprinkled in your eyes, you just wake up in your bed the next morning and you don't remember a thing.

I thought it would be different, being an elf. Better, I suppose. At least, I thought I would be better at it.

And then there's Lapland. I mean, don't get me wrong, it's a lovely place an' all, but it's just, well, it's not home I suppose. It's actually quite a long way away from where I live with my family: my parents – us elves call them Mama and Papa – and my little sister, Starling, who I never thought I'd miss on account of the way she chews the heads off my dolls and rips pages out of my favourite books. Mama says she doesn't do it on purpose. It's only because she's a baby. It's funny the things you miss. Like our house and the way you can see the mountains – snowy and tall – from my bedroom in the attic. The mountains look like Baked Alaska, which happens to be my favourite dessert.

Us elves, we can't go home for Christmas. That's the busiest time of the whole year, as you can imagine. Getting Father Christmas ready for the trip. Making the toys. Packing the sleigh, tight as a drum. Some children think we pack all the toys on the sleigh at the one time, but that's not true. Father Christmas does it one continent at a time. Australia first, then Asia, Africa, Europe and all the way over the Atlantic Ocean to America. He doesn't go to the Antarctic. There aren't any children there. When he's finished one continent, he returns to the workshop and we pack more toys onto the sleigh and recharge it with energy from the Laughometre and polish Rudolph's nose. It's true that Rudolph's nose is bright red, but it can get a bit dusty, especially when he flies over places like the Sahara Desert, so we have to give it a bit of a polish and shine.

Of course, it doesn't take Father Christmas as long as it would take you or I to travel around the world. He uses a special kind of magic for that. Even if I knew what it was, I wouldn't be allowed to tell you. It's a secret, you see.

❄ ♥ ❄

So here I am, in the workshop, trying to concentrate on fairy dust. It's Christmas Eve. The busiest day of the year. Nobody talks, not even Wishes who talks in her sleep. Glint and Sparkle concentrate on putting the finishing touches on the furniture for the dolls' houses. Shadow and Rainbow blow up the tyres of the toy cars and trucks and buses. Their cheeks puff up like red balloons.

And then it happens. There's a surge of activity in the Laughometre. This is not unusual, especially on Christmas Eve when children laugh – and giggle, chortle, chuckle and even gurgle – a lot more than they usually do. When a surge occurs, the Laughometre bulges as it shoots all the extra laughs into the bit of the machine that we call 'The Compressor', which is just a fancy way of explaining how the extra laughs get squashed flat and stacked away neatly with the other laughs. Usually the machine stops bulging and we all get back to work.

But not this time.

This time, the Laughometre bulges and keeps on bulging. Not only does it bulge, it coughs, splutters, shakes and shudders before the blinking lights fade like stars at dawn and the machine falls silent. In fact, the entire workshop falls silent, as all the other machines – the Wishing Well, the Stairway to Heaven, the Flower Tower, all of them – slow down before they stop altogether and the whole workshop plunges into darkness.

You might not know this, but elves are afraid of the dark. It's just that we're not used to it. Even when the sun goes down in Lapland, the sky is still lit like a candle with the Aurora Borealis: the Northern Lights. You might think that the Northern Lights look like clusters of fairies in the sky, in dresses of green and red and yellow and white and pink, fluttering their fairy wings and dancing their fairy dances. Well, you'd be right.

In the few seconds it takes the fairies – who sleep during the day – to wake up and get their wings fluttering fast enough to leak their colours into the darkness of the workshop, everybody panics, running in circles with their pointed green hats pressed against their bright green eyes, which is the thing that elves do when they are frightened. As for me, I stand still and close my eyes and think about Mama and Papa and even Starling and my attic bedroom at the top of our little house and the mountains that I can see from there – snowy and tall – like Baked Alaska. This is how I stop feeling afraid. It works. I open my eyes. I feel my way towards the Laughometre and when I get there, I run my hands along it. I feel nothing but a low rumbling deep inside the machine. I look around and pick up a fluttering fairy, holding her close to the machine, trying to see where the problem might be. It's hard to concentrate with the noise of hundreds of panicking elves all around, but I know I have to. It's Christmas Eve. The most important day of the year. And then I see them. A huge knot of giggles trapped in the pipe that leads to the chortles. I can still hear them giggling but only just. There is no time to lose. The pipe containing them looks like it's about to burst any minute. Even as I stand there, more laughs crash down the mouth of the pipe where they collect before they are sorted into their groups. I throw myself in front of the opening and the incoming laughs bounce against my chest, my head, my

arms, before dribbling down my body and landing in a heap on the floor. It will only be a matter of minutes before they pick themselves up and try to enter the Laughometre again. Laughs are very determined, you know.

'Think,' I tell myself. 'Think.'

It's hard to think when you're being bombarded by laughter. But I do manage to have a thought and it's this: I need to clear the blockage of giggles in the chortles pipe. As more and more fairies flicker and flutter about the workshop, the light improves and I see Glint standing beside the Rainbow Riot Machine with his green hat held over his green eyes.

'Glint,' I shout. 'Over here. Quickly.'

'It's too dark. I can't see. I'm scared.'

'It's not. The fairy lights are on. Open your eyes.'

Glint peeks through a narrow gap in his fingers. 'What are you doing?' he shouts as I duck my head to avoid a particularly loud chuckle.

'I need you to put your hand down the chortle pipe and pull the giggles out.'

'Why don't you do it?' Glint asks, his voice wobbling like a jelly.

'I have to stand here and make sure no other laughs get into the machine until we've cleared the blockage,' I explain, sneezing as two gurgles glance against my nose.

'Ok,' Glint says, lowering his hands. 'I'll try.'

He runs to the pipe and tries to push his hand inside. But it won't fit. He can't do it. Nor can Sparkle, Shadow or Rainbow who see what's happening and come over to the Laughometre to help.

'It's going to blow,' Sparkle screams looking at the machine with tears in her eyes. 'Christmas will be ruined. Forever.'

'Wait. You're the smallest, Robin,' Glint says to me. 'You should try.'

He takes my place, pressing his body tight against the main pipe where he is immediately splattered by a cluster of giggles, chuckles and a few belly laughs.

'Ouch,' he says, but he stays there all the same. I run to the chortles pipe and try to squeeze my hand inside it. But the pipe is narrow. I curl my hand into the tightest fist that I can make and try again. It fits! I ease it down the pipe until my fingers touch the knot of giggles. They feel soft and light, like feathers. I pick them out, one by one, and I don't stop until the pipe is clear. Glint steps away from the main pipe and the laughs on the floor pick themselves up, dust themselves down and charge into the machine. We all hold our breath.

'Well done Robin. You fixed it.'

I look up and gasp, the way anyone would if they looked up and saw Father Christmas standing there beside them, smiling his big old Father Christmas smile. I've seen him before. Once. When I first arrived. But still. There's something about him that makes me gasp. It could be the twinkle in the bright blueness of his eyes. His beautiful red suit with the snow-white trim. His long, curly beard. His shiny black boots. I can see my face in those boots, that's how shiny they are.

A hush falls across the workshop. Even the machines, working again, are quieter.

'Greetings my little elves,' he says and even though he has a lovely soft, low voice, everybody hears him. Everybody looks up. Everybody gasps. He smiles his smile that is as warm as one of Mama's pancakes fresh off the pan.

He turns back to me. 'You've saved Christmas Robin,' he says. 'Thank you.'

'Eh, you're welcome,' is all I can think of to say.

'I want you to be in charge of the Laughometre in future,' Father Christmas says. There is a gasp from the other elves. And from Miss Pritchett who is standing beside me now.

'But … but … Father Christmas. Robin is the youngest elf in the workshop,' Miss Pritchett tells him.

'And the smallest,' a group of elves mutter behind his back. Father Christmas turns to them and smiles. 'She is brave and resourceful,' he tells them and even though I don't know what resourceful means, it sounds like something good, the way he says it.

'She has saved Christmas, not just for the children but

for us as well. Where would we be without Christmas?' Everybody takes a moment to think about an answer to this question. But there is none. Instead, the workshop elves charge towards me and for a moment I am frightened. They reach for me with their hands and hoist me on their shoulders, carrying me around the room like a trophy, cheering and laughing.

'Well done Robin!' cries Flint.

'You've saved the day!' roars Copper.

'You're our hero, Tiny!' says Butch and the way he says it sounds great. Fantastic in fact.

I think about next week, when I am home for the holidays. Telling Mama and Papa and Starling all about Christmas Eve in Santa's workshop. I can't wait. But for now, sitting on the shoulders of my fellow elves, while I'm still the smallest elf, it feels like I'm on top of the world.

The Other Bear

JUDI CURTIN

It was late on Christmas night in the little house at the edge of the forest. The children were sleepy and their tummies were full of chocolate.

'Time for bed,' said Dad.

'No,' said Beth. 'Five minutes more, please.'

'Granny can tell us a story,' said William.

'Just one story and then straight to bed,' said Dad, and he settled down to listen too.

Granny smiled and began: 'Once upon a time there were three bears. The first bear was called Clever Bear.'

'Why?' asked William.

'Because he was the cleverest bear in the whole world. The second bear was called Brave Bear, because he was the bravest bear in the whole world. And the third bear – well he

wasn't particularly good at anything so everyone just called him The Other Bear – and he really, really hated that.'

'Where did the bears live?' asked William.

'Why, in the forest just over there,' said Granny, pointing through the window.

The wind suddenly howled in the trees, and Beth shivered.

'There aren't any bears in that forest,' said Dad.

'Just because you've never seen them, that doesn't mean they're not there,' said Granny.

'Can we get on with the story?' asked William.

'One cold dark winter's night,' said Granny, 'the three bears were curled up in their cave. Clever Bear was asleep, dreaming of very hard maths problems. Brave Bear was asleep, dreaming of fighting fierce, scary dragons. Only The Other Bear was awake and he was thinking about – well, nothing very much.

'Suddenly, there was a strange jingly sound outside. The Other Bear crept to the edge of the cave and peeped out, and what do you think he saw?'

'What?' asked Beth, with shining eyes.

'He saw Santa Claus with all his reindeer and his sleigh stacked high with presents,' said Granny.

'Who could this man in the funny red suit be?' wondered The Other Bear.

'How come the bear didn't recognise Santa?' asked William.

'Because Santa doesn't come to bears,' said Granny.

'I'm glad I'm not a bear,' said Beth, hugging her new doll more tightly to her chest.

'Anyway,' said Granny. 'Even though he was a little bit afraid, The Other Bear was a very polite little bear.

'"Can I help you?" he said to Santa.

'"We took a short cut," said Santa. "But Rudolph's Sat Nav isn't working with all these trees, and we seem to be lost. I don't suppose you know the way out of here?"

'The Other Bear smiled. "Just follow me," he said.

'The path was long and twisty. The air was so chilly that icicles began to grow on The Other Bear's fur, and he started to turn blue with the cold. Even though it was so very dark, the reindeer were easily able to follow the eerie blue glow, and soon they were at the edge of the forest.

'"Thank you so much," said Santa. "You've saved Christmas and I think you deserve a present."

'The Other Bear beamed. He'd never been given a present before.

'"How would you like a big box of Lego?" asked Santa.

'The Other Bear held up his big clumsy paws.

'"Hmm … maybe not," said Santa.

'"How about this great new games console?"

'"No electricity in my cave," said The Other Bear sadly. Then he saw the huge pot of honey on the front seat of the sleigh and his eyes lit up.

"'Sorry," said Santa. "Mrs Claus asked me to pick that up at the supermarket and I'm in big trouble if I get home without it." He looked at his watch. "I don't mean to be rude, but I still have thirty-seven countries to visit. Why don't you tell me your name and address, and I'll send you on a present next week, when I'm not so busy?"

'The Other Bear put his head down, ashamed. "I don't have a proper name," he said. "No one ever bothered to give me one."

"'Well, that's it," said Santa. "I'll give you a present of a name."

'The Other Bear smiled shyly. "I'd like that," he said.

"'I'm glad that's sorted," said Santa jumping into the seat of his sleigh.

"'How about Teddy? Teddy's a good solid name for a bear."

'The Other Bear shook his head slowly.

"'Paddington?" suggested Santa.

'The Other Bear shook his head again.

'Santa turned back to his reindeer. "Come on guys," he said. "Help me out here. Think of a name for this fine bear."

"'Rumpelstiltskin," suggested Donner, who liked fairy tales.

"'Blitzen," suggested Blitzen, who was a bit vain.

"'Bare Bear," suggested Prancer, who thought he was very clever.

'Each time, The Other Bear shook his head.

"'I don't mean to be ungrateful," he said. "But as I've waited so long for a name, when I get one, it needs to be the best name ever."

'Suddenly, Rudolph smiled. He leaned over and whispered in Santa's ear. Santa smiled. Santa leaned over and whispered in The Other Bear's ear. The Other Bear smiled.

"'Perfect," he said.

'So Santa flew off to deliver the rest of his presents, and Bert the Blue-Bottomed Bear ambled back to his cave. His name mightn't sound as good as Rudolph the Red-Nosed Reindeer, but that didn't matter. Bert the Blue-Bottomed Bear still went on to be famous all around the world. The End.'

Granny sat back in her chair and folded her arms.

'Bert the Blue-Bottomed Bear isn't famous,' protested Beth. 'I've never even heard of him before.'

'You just made him up,' said William.

Granny didn't answer, and as the children made their way upstairs to bed, no one noticed the eerie blue glow coming from the edge of the forest, as Bert the Blue-Bottomed Bear went for his nightly stroll.

Soon everyone in the house was sound asleep, and Beth, William, Dad, Granny and Bert the Blue-Bottomed Bear all lived happily ever after.

26

Mr Frog, Santa Claus and the House with No Chimney

CATHY KELLY

A month before Christmas, Mum hurries into the kitchen waving a letter and shrieking: 'We're going to spend Christmas with Aunt Helen! Isn't that fabulous?'

Me and Ben stare at each other in horror.

'Christmas –' I say.

'– in Aunt Helen's house?' finishes Ben.

Me and Ben are twins. We finish each other's sentences. Twins do this. Grown-ups think it's very strange. Kids in our class – we are seven and three-quarters – think it's cool.

'Her house is weird,' says Ben. 'So weird.'

Aunt Helen's house is white. Even her cat, CoochieCoo, is white. You have to take your shoes off at the door.

Dad says CoochieCoo probably has to wear special cat shoes outside so that when he comes in he can take them off and not get dirt on the carpet.

'Stevie, she has no television,' whispered Ben to me.

I am Stevie. Mum and Dad only call me Stephen when I've done something wrong.

'Stephen, how did the ant farm escape?'

The ants were bored. I wanted to see what they would do if they were out. They loved it. Mum didn't.

Mum wants us to go to Aunt Helen's because Mum has a broken leg. She has to walk with crutches.

'How can I organise Christmas dinner with a leg in plaster?' I heard her say this to Dad.

Her plaster is cool. It's pink and we got to write our names and draw pictures on it.

She fell into a hole while she was walking Mr Frog, our dog. Mr Frog was very good and sat on her to keep her warm until help arrived. He is a hero dog!

I suddenly realise that Mr Frog won't be allowed to go to Aunt Helen's house.

'Mr Frog won't be able to come for Christmas!' I shriek.

Mr Frog has never been in Aunt Helen's house. He is always dirty. He loves mud almost as much as he loves dog treats.

When Aunt Helen comes to our house, she says, 'lovely dog'. Then she moves away from him. Kids notice these things.

Our house is great. It is messy but we love it. I can wear my shoes inside.

'Mr Frog can stay in the kennels,' Mum says.

Me and Ben look at each other. We cannot have Christmas in a house with no television, no shoes on and no Mr Frog. We love him and have had him since he was a puppy. And once he nearly ate a whole chair.

And then I remember the worst thing: Aunt Helen has no fireplace. She has a pretend fire in a television screen where the fireplace should be. How can Santa Claus deliver our presents to a television screen fire? This is a DISASTER!

In our bedroom, we sit on our beds and think. Our bedroom is blue and purple. Ben's side is blue with dinosaurs and my side is purple with planets.

'I don't like Aunt Helen,' says Ben crossly.

'You can't say that,' I say.

'Yes, I can.'

'Can't.'

'Can.'

'She likes clean things too much,' I say.

Aunt Helen is nice and gives us money for presents. We like this. But she does not understand Christmas. No fireplace for Santa Claus, no television and no dogs. That is what Christmas is about.

Aunt Helen is Mum's older sister. She has mad black hair and wears red lipstick. Mum has no other family except for us and Dad. She likes spending time with Aunt Helen. But it is hard to be clean always.

'We need a plan,' I say.

'Can we go to Aunt Helen's house this Saturday?' I ask Mum.

She looks surprised.

On Saturdays, me and Ben like to go to the park with Mr Frog and play. Our friend Posy is collecting strange weeds. She often comes to the park with us too. She has a lot of weeds now. They are sometimes smelly. But she likes them. Sometimes Mr Frog steals them and runs off with weeds hanging out of his mouth. Even Posy laughs when he does this.

'Yes, we could go to Helen's house –' Mum says cautiously.

'Goodie!' I say.

I really want to go to the park but this is an emergency.

Aunt Helen has a new table for Christmas lunch. It looks like an ordinary table to me. Aunt Helen and Mum think it is amazing. They talk about it for ages and walk around it a lot. This is useful because me and Ben can do our planning.

We examine the television fireplace. I pull it and so does Ben but it won't come off the wall. There is no way Santa Claus will be able to squeeze out of there.

We go upstairs to check the bedrooms. We stayed once before for a sleepover, but only for one night. Aunt Helen put us in a silver and white bedroom with a big white bed. A huge silver light hangs over the bed. I was afraid it would fall on the bed and squish us.

The big light is still there. We could be squished for Christmas. It would be no fun.

'We need a plan,' I say.

Me and Ben count our pocket money.

I am very good at saving. I have twenty-one euro and seventeen cents. Ben has one euro and no cents. He likes the teddy grabbing machines. He has only ever won one teddy.

'Is that much money enough for Christmas things to eat?' Ben asks me. We look at all our money.

'Oh yes,' I say. 'Loads.'

A lady in the supermarket asks us where our Mum is. We have Dad's calculator and are adding up all the things we put in the trolley.

'Mum is here —' I say.

'— somewhere,' Ben adds.

This is not true. Mum is at home. She thinks we are in Posy's back garden next door looking at her weeds.

We have decided to do the Christmas shopping ourselves. Mum won't hurt her broken leg and we will not have to go to Aunt Helen's. It's a brilliant plan.

We have a lot of biscuits in our trolley. Ben wants pizza but it is too expensive.

Turkeys are really heavy. They also cost a lot of money. We do not get one. I do not like turkey anyway. Mince pies are very cheap. We put in two packs. I add in fizzy drinks last. The ones Mum won't let us have.

At the checkout, a man in a suit like a policeman stands in front of us.

'Where is your mother, boys?' he asks.

Oops.

Dad can't stop laughing when he comes home from work.

'It is not funny!' Mum shouts.

Mr Frog runs and hides under the kitchen table.

Dad tries to stop laughing. His mouth twitches.

'We wanted to buy Christmas food so Mum didn't have to –' I say.

'– and we wouldn't have to go to Aunt Helen's,' adds Ben. 'She has no television –'

'– or chimney,' I say.

'– or room for Mr Frog.'

Mr Frog's big tail thumps under the table.

Aunt Helen stays in our spare bedroom for Christmas. We painted it white specially. Ben and me helped. Painting is very messy.

CoochieCoo and Mr Frog sort of like each other. Except that CoochieCoo hisses at Mr Frog.

We are going to leave mince pies and milk out for Santa Claus on Christmas Eve. Dad is going to put them on the mantelpiece in case Mr Frog gets them.

It's going to be the best Christmas ever.

MONDAY 13 DECEMBER

NIALL QUINN

Dear Santa,

It's me again, Mikey Quinn age seven and a quarter from Perrystown, writing another letter to you but this time it's not my letter. It's for Mam and Dad. They don't know about it yet.

I'm also giving you my painting of the Reindeer World Cup which Miss Murphy thinks is great as she says I show promise as a footballer and an artist – Aisling helped me with it. So please pass it on to Dasher, Dancer, Prancer, Vixen, Comet, Cupid, Donner, Rudolph and the other reindeer who I can't remember … I hope they like the special North Pole jerseys we designed for them.

I still want that red Flicker, the football and a surprise please, but I'm not allowed to ask for a mobile phone as Mam says 'No way José' (even though she knows my name) and then she says she doesn't care if my cousin Sam already has one. I've just been helping again with the big Christmas tidy up and found those two old mobile phones in the bottom drawer for our Jack & Jill school box to help sick children get nurses at home – so if you find any phones on your travels Santa, please post them to Jack & Jill in Dublin. When I grow up I'm going to send them lots of old mobiles.

Hopefully you're OK with my last letter Santa and I'm still on the good list? So sorry for giving Aisling the paint box after we'd finished the Reindeer World Cup. She got her two friends Eve and Orlaith in to play Showhouse in the hall and Mam's not happy with the big crooked rainbow they painted right beside the coat stand. Sorry, sorry, sorry, sorry, sorry multiplied by a million Santa. I've put the paintbox up again and Mam says I can help Dad with painting the hall later tonight – now also on the To Do list.

So I'm getting busy, busy just like all the grown-ups at Christmas, except Nana who is still lots of fun and always has time to tell us a story and lets us bake apple tarts and chocolate-covered Smartie buns.

Mam and Dad did our To Do list last night and it's eight pages long and we're having a family competition for ticking off the most jobs with only eleven days to go – Mam's in the lead of course, Dad is second and me and Aisling are Paddy Last. Suppose it serves me right after the Rainbow Paint job!!

Our teacher, Miss Murphy, says that Christmas time is all about giving and doing nice things for your family and friends and helping out at home like big boys and girls, just like the Wise Men visiting the Baby Jesus in Bethlehem. And not asking Santa for too many presents. Did you know that Ben Murray has fifteen things on his Santa list, but teacher says we should ask you for just one thing because you have a whole planet to deliver to and that's a lot of stuff, even with the magic time dust. Hope you're OK with my three things? The Flicker is very light and the football won't take up much room – I'll leave the surprise up to you and that can be very, very, small too.

My question Santa is about the magic dust you have and whether it could do magic cleaning in double quick time as well? With all these things on the To Do list, I don't think Mam and Dad have any time to do the good stuff at Christmas and that's why I'm writing. Mam and Dad are definitely on the Good List I know. They're always doing good stuff for me and Aisling and they deserve a Big Big Surprise.

So when you come down the chimney on Christmas Eve (or maybe you can throw some down beforehand) can you sprinkle some magic dust on the house that washes the windows, floors and bathroom, cooks the gigantic turkey and the fancy roast potatoes and carrots and stuffing, clears out the drawers and tidies the toys away neatly and gets the trifle done with the lovely sprinkles on top and all the other stuff on the eight pages. I know you can do it Santa and maybe you could do Ben Murray's house too, especially if he gets his list down from fifteen to one or two.

You see Mam and Dad are just so busy all the time and me and Aisling just want them to have fun on Christmas morning with us, so that we're not rushing out the door to Mass with Mam giving out and Dad shaking his head as usual. Nana says Mam loves Christmas really and when she was small she played more than any child on her road, for hours and hours with her doll's house. Uncle Phil says Dad was always first down in the morning to see what presents you'd brought in the Good Old Days and his favourite was his Red Train Set. What happens to grown-ups at Christmas is a bit sad I think. The bigger you get the busier you are, until some day you're just too busy to talk or to play.

I know from talking to my friends in school that all Mams and Dads go a bit doo-lally at Christmas and they all write lists with no play time on them, ever. Why is that? Why don't they remember the Good Old Days as Uncle Phil says?

Sorry, have to go for a minute, Mam's calling me.

It's OK Santa. No need for To Do magic dust at all. Mam and Dad read my letter and Mam got a bit sad and then started to laugh and kept hugging me. I've got to go now, as we're all heading out for a walk around to that big house on the Green with all the amazing lights and zillions of Santas and Snowmen. You know, the one you can see from the aeroplanes and your sleigh. It's really cool and we've wanted to go for ages. Mam tore up the To Do list and said this letter was the best Christmas present ever. You must have sprinkled some magic dust on the house while I was downstairs.

Thanks Santa and make sure you take an extra hot chocolate and marshmallow rest from the workshop tonight and maybe the reindeer can play four-a-side during their break.

Love

Mikey

PS: Say hi to Blitzen for me – Dad reminded me of his name.

THE MAGIC OF CHRISTMAS TIME

KATE GAYNOR

It was mid-December and Cathy and Ben were already looking forward to their Christmas holidays.

'I can hardly wait for school to be finished,' said Cathy to her brother Ben as they climbed the stairs of the big yellow school bus.

'In less than two weeks Santa will be visiting our house, can you believe it?'

'I know!' said Ben, smiling as they took their seats. 'I sent my letter weeks ago!'

When the bus pulled up to the crossroads, the children waved goodbye to their friends and began the short walk to the cottage at the end of the lane.

The hedgerows along the lane were heavy with frost

and the ice crunched under their winter boots as they walked.

Ben pushed open the big red front door of the cottage just as Mum bustled past in her slippers. 'Oh, hi you two,' she said. 'Come and help me set the table, Joe has finally fallen asleep and I have a million things to do before your Dad gets home.'

Joe was Cathy and Ben's little brother; he was only three months old, but since he had arrived the whole house had been turned upside-down and Mum never seemed to have time for anything anymore.

'If only there were a few extra hours in the day,' said Mum, as she hurried around the kitchen preparing dinner.

Later that evening, Dad, Ben and Cathy sat around the big wooden table in the kitchen to discuss Mum's Christmas present.

'Mum has been so busy and tired lately, so we need to get her something really special to cheer her up,' said Dad.

'Well how about a new bag for work?' suggested Ben. 'The one she has now is broken at the handle.'

'That's a silly idea,' said Cathy. 'Mum doesn't want to be reminded of work on Christmas morning.'

40

'Fine,' said Ben angrily, 'you come up with something then.'

'Well how about a new pair of slippers?' suggested Cathy.

'That's what we got her last year,' moaned Ben. 'We need something that will really cheer her up.'

'I know,' said Dad, 'why don't we all take a trip into town and see if we can find something in the shops that she will really like.'

'Great idea Dad!' said Ben and Cathy together.

And so it was on Christmas Eve, Dad, Cathy and Ben took the bus into town in search of a really special present for Mum.

There was always an air of excitement in town on Christmas Eve. Shops were busy with last minute shoppers loaded with bags and the streets were bustling with carol singers and friends wishing each other a 'Merry Christmas'.

The lights on the big fir tree twinkled and shone and the windows of the shops sparkled with festive decorations.

'OK you two,' said Dad, 'here's some money, why don't you try looking for something for Mum in one of the shops nearby and I'll meet you under the Christmas tree in an hour. Be sure to stay close, keep track of time and don't be late!'

With the money safely stored away in Ben's deepest pocket, the children set off along the main street, peering in each of the beautifully decorated Christmas windows as they went.

In the brightly lit windows along the main street there were all sorts of wonderful toys and presents on display and Ben and Cathy almost lost track of time as they walked along!

'Oh Ben, let's go this way,' said Cathy as they passed a little cobbled street that was festooned with fairy lights overhead.

'I don't think I've ever seen this shop before,' said Ben, stopping suddenly on the cobbles to push his nose up against the murky glass of a tiny wooden window.

The Time Keeper – was painted in red letters above the door.

'Come on let's go in,' said Cathy.

Ben hesitated. 'It looks a little dark inside – do you think we should?'

'Of course!' said Cathy, who loved adventures. 'It looks like the sort of place that might be perfect for finding something special for Mum.'

The children pushed open the shop door and a silver bell rang overhead.

As they stepped inside it was almost impossible to move around as every surface was covered in old toys, bikes and painted wooden ornaments. Cobwebs hung in every corner and a silvery dust covered every shelf. A faint smell of cinnamon biscuits and hot cocoa filled the air.

Suddenly, a black cat darted across their path and both children let out a loud scream.

'Oh, I'm sorry children,' chuckled the man who appeared as if by magic behind the counter. 'That's Claws, he's terribly friendly. There's no need to be afraid.'

Cathy and Ben could barely see because the light was so dim in the tiny shop. From what they could make out the man was wearing a large red overcoat and a white beard covered most of his round face. Peering out from behind his glasses were two twinkling black eyes.

'So, what can I help you two with?' he asked kindly.

'Well, we're looking for something special for our Mum,' said Cathy. 'She's been so busy and tired since baby Joe arrived; we wanted to get her something special to really cheer her up.'

'Yes,' Ben joined in, 'Mum says there just aren't enough hours in the day anymore. We're hoping on Christmas Day she'll have the time to enjoy the best present ever!'

'Time is a funny thing you know,' said the man behind the counter. 'It can catch you out without you even knowing. And no one can stop it passing, not even for all the money in the world … Well, no one can stop it apart from one man that is.'

'And who might that be?' whispered Ben and Cathy in unison.

'Well Santa Claus of course!' laughed the man behind the counter with a deep belly laugh that made the tiny ornaments on the shelves shake. 'Santa has the magic of Christmas time – how else would he deliver presents to every boy and girl in the world in just one night?

'You know,' continued the man, 'I think I have the perfect present for your Mum.'

And from underneath the counter he took a tiny black box, which he placed carefully on the counter where the children could see. Suddenly, the box popped open and inside on a red velvet cushion was the most beautiful watch the children had ever seen.

It had an oval pearl face that captured all the colours of the rainbow. The delicate straps were lined with tiny stars that glistened around the edges like fairy lights.

'We'll take it!' said Cathy. She beamed as she quickly handed the man the money Dad had given them earlier. 'Thank you and Merry Christmas,' Ben and Cathy called back as they hurried out of the shop and onto the cobbled street again.

As they stepped onto the street they could hardly believe their eyes, every surface as far as they could see was covered in thick, white snow.

'How long were we in there?' asked Ben, his eyes wide open in disbelief.

'I really don't know!' said Cathy. 'But can you believe the snow? It really feels like Christmas now!'

The children hurried back through the crowds, eager to meet Dad and tell him about the shop they had found.

'But I know every shop in town,' said Dad, looking puzzled. 'And I'm sure I've never seen or heard of that place – The Time Keeper. I think you both must be mistaken.'

Cathy looked at Ben and winked, 'OK Dad, you're probably right, let's just go home and get ready for Santa.'

Later that night, Ben and Cathy placed the little black box under the tree with a red ribbon around it and a note: 'To Mum, love Ben & Cathy, Happy Christmas.'

The next morning the children awoke to a winter wonderland. The garden of their cottage was frosty white and the snow glistened in the Christmas morning sunshine.

As they hurried downstairs, Mum, as usual, was already up. But instead of rushing around she was sipping a cup of tea toasting her toes in front of a roaring fire.

'Happy Christmas Cathy and Ben,' she said with a big smile. 'Come on let's open your presents and then we'll make the biggest snowman ever in the garden!'

'But are you sure you have time Mum?' asked Ben. 'Are you not going to be too busy today?'

'Yes, we really don't mind building the snowman on our own,' said Cathy.

'I'm never too busy for my two favourite people,' said Mum as she hugged them both tightly. 'And besides, it's strange but suddenly I feel like I have all the time in the world! Now come on, let's get out into the snow!'

Ben and Cathy could hardly believe it! They both hurried to the hall to wrap up in their hats and scarves, but just as they did something caught Cathy's eye. Mum was already wearing her Christmas present. The beautiful watch glistened and danced in the morning sunlight.

A noise from the roof made Cathy look out through the frosted glass window, and in the distance she thought she caught a glimpse of a red coat, a sleigh and reindeers.

'Come on you two, let's go!' laughed Mum, and Cathy and Ben pulled opened the big red door and ran out into the snow.

A PRECOCIOUS CHILD

MAEVE BINCHY

When I was young and spoiled and indulged, instead of being old and spoiled and indulged, I decided late one Christmas Eve that I was going to cancel all previous letters to Santa Claus and ask him for a doll's house.

Laboriously and apologetically I wrote all this to himself and put it up the chimney and retired happily, leaving confusion and sadness, as my parents were afraid it was too late for Santa to get my letter and to bring a doll's house.

A child's Christmas couldn't be ruined, they told each other, so they tried to make one. For hours and hours, I believe, they laboured on a big box and painted it white and drew windows on it and stuck on chimneys that kept falling off. One of the few rows of their married life developed over the inability to construct a simple thing like a doll's house.

'Boys should have learned carpentry at school,' said my mother in despair as the front of the house caved in yet again.

'Women should know about toys,' countered my father as he got out the glue pot once more.

Then they thought about straw and making a doll's house, Hawaiian style, but this might not be a good idea in case I hadn't heard of Polynesian houses.

'With all the money we pay at that expensive school, they should have taught her that,' said my father. But the straw was damp anyway, so that was abandoned.

A doll's igloo with cotton wool as snow was considered and abandoned. A doll's tepee seemed a good idea if they could paint a doll up as an Indian to go with it. But it required bark, skins or canvas, and so they had to give that up, too, since they had been thinking of making it with a sheet.

They ruminated wistfully about my younger sister then, and how she, easier to please in life, would be delighted with a rattle or a teddy bear or even nothing at all.

'To be fair,' said my father, 'she is only two. Maeve is six.'

'I wonder is it normal for a six-year-old to want a doll's house anyway,' said my mother. So they had another hour looking up 'Normal-Six-Year-Olds' in Dr Spock or its equivalent, decided it was boringly normal and inconvenient, and went back to work.

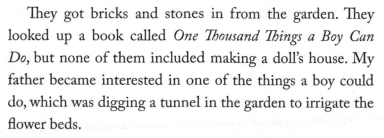

They got bricks and stones in from the garden. They looked up a book called *One Thousand Things a Boy Can Do*, but none of them included making a doll's house. My father became interested in one of the things a boy could do, which was digging a tunnel in the garden to irrigate the flower beds.

'That's all we need on Christmas Day,' said my mother wearily, 'for the neighbours to see you irrigating the flower beds with tunnels.'

It was nearly dawn when they eventually gave up and hoped their fat cherub – who was asleep with no idea of anything being amiss – would not be too disappointed with Santa's present.

❄ ♥ ❄

It was morning, and with shining eyes I was beating on them, begging them to wake up. After only two hours' sleep this wasn't easy for them to do. They showed great alarm. Was I going to threaten to leave home! Were there tears and tantrums which would spoil the day for everyone! Not at all.

'You'll never believe it,' I said. 'Santa Claus wrote me a note. In his own writing on a lovely new blackboard:

Dear Maeve,

Your chimney is too narrow and I can't get the doll's house down it. Please do not be upset, It will arrive as an extra gift sometime in January. You have been a good girl. All the reindeer are asking for you.

Love from Santa Claus

'It's very valuable. Nobody has seen Santa Claus' writing before. We'll have to show it to everyone. We might lend it to a museum.'

It was a good Christmas, like all our Christmases together were; the only thing that makes me sad at this time of the year is that I may have forgotten to tell them that ... but perhaps they knew.

LITTLE TOMMY GOES HOME

YVONNE CASSIDY

It was Christmas Eve and excitement was in the air in Santa's workshop. Beep and Blink, the race cars, were chasing each other and getting in Elfie's way as he tried to sweep the floor. Across the room a little green hippo called Tommy was playing snap with his friend Beany the frog. They were finding it hard to concentrate because of the argument between the teddy bears and the dolls.

'I hope I get a boy,' a small brown bear called Fraser said. 'Boys take you outside on adventures. They climb trees.'

'I like trees,' said Herman, a black teddy with a deep voice and a leather nose.

'Well, I'm glad I'm going to a little girl,' said Holly the doll. 'Girls buy you lots of clothes. I've so many dresses already, I'm not sure what to wear tonight!'

Holly had already changed four times that day and the two teddies laughed. Holly turned her back on them and stomped off, her yellow woollen ringlets shaking as she walked.

'It's your turn Tommy,' said Beany, hopping from one card to another. 'We don't have all night.'

The clock said it was eight o'clock. Santa had already left with the toys for China. Tommy and Beany were going on the sleigh to Ireland and they were leaving at midnight.

'Four more hours,' Tommy said.

'Are you OK Tommy?' asked Beany. 'You didn't eat your snow pie at lunchtime. You're not scared about meeting your new owner are you?'

'Scared?' said Tommy. 'Of course not!'

Elfie was sweeping up next to them and he stopped to lean on his brush. He was the oldest of Santa's elves, the one in charge of checking the lists twice. He knew everything there was to know about Christmas.

'Lots of toys feel scared on Christmas Eve,' he said. 'But there's nothing to worry about, you know.'

Tommy didn't know at all. It seemed to him there was a lot to worry about. He worried about leaving Beany and Elfie behind. He worried about going to live with people he didn't know. He worried because the other hippos made fun of him because he was green and not grey or brown like them. He hadn't been able to sleep last night worrying about it all.

'I know you'll love your new home Little Tommy,' Elfie said, his blue eyes twinkling.

'Why do you always call me Little Tommy?' Tommy asked. 'I'm bigger than Beany and he's just Beany.'

'Wait and see Little Tommy,' said Elfie. 'Just wait and see.'

At midnight the elves loaded the toys for Ireland into red bags. Beany and Tommy made sure they went in the same bag. Inside it was dark and snug and the toys started to fall asleep, all except Tommy. Tommy was awake, listening to everything: the swoosh of the sleigh through the sky, the bump as it landed on each roof and Santa's clucking noise to get the reindeer started again.

Bit by bit, the bag emptied – Beep and Blink, Ruben the giraffe, even Beany all found new homes. Just as Tommy was about to fall asleep, the bag opened wide and he saw Santa smiling at him.

'Time to see your new home Little Tommy,' said Santa.

Before Tommy could ask why Santa called him Little Tommy as well, they were both outside on the roof of a house. Tommy could see the moon and he remembered Elfie saying it was the same moon they could see from the North Pole. It was warm and safe in Santa's arms and Tommy wasn't scared at all whooshing down the chimney.

In the sitting-room Tommy saw a pine tree that was covered in lights. The tree smelled like the North Pole. Elfie had told him that was why humans put trees up at Christmas, so the toys wouldn't be homesick.

❄ ♥ ❄

Tommy expected Santa to leave him under the tree but he didn't. Instead, he opened a door and took him into a hall and up some stairs.

'Where are we going?' asked Tommy.

'Sssh!' said Santa. 'We don't want to wake her up.'

On the landing there were three doors. Santa pushed one of them open and Tommy could see a little girl in bed, sound asleep. It was only then he realised that he was the only toy in Santa's arms. This little girl had asked only for him.

'She only ever asks for one toy,' whispered Santa, as if he could read Tommy's mind. 'Every year, one special toy to join the family.'

At first Tommy thought Santa meant the little girl's human family, but then he turned around and saw what Santa was looking at. Lined up beside the bed was a row of toys. But they weren't just any toys. They were all hippos. And they weren't just any hippos, they were all green hippos, just like Tommy. The one at the end was ten times Tommy's size, with a big smile to match.

'Hello Little Tommy,' he said. 'I'm Big Tommy.'

'Welcome home!' said the hippo next to him, 'I'm Big Tammy and this is Little Tammy!'

Little Tammy was a girl hippo, the same size as Tommy. She smiled and waved a green paw. At first Tommy didn't know how they knew his name, or why they looked like him. But then he remembered what Santa had said and that they were his new family.

'Hello,' he whispered.

'You'll have lots to talk about in the morning,' said Santa, 'but for now, this little hippo needs some sleep.'

Tommy realised suddenly how very, very tired he was and how long it was since he had slept. Santa gently lifted up the little girl's arm and slid Tommy in underneath it. She hugged him and he felt warm and safe, just like in Santa's arms. Little Tommy took one last look at his new family, before he closed his eyes and fell fast asleep.

THE HOUND
AND THE HATCHET

TOM O'NEILL

Auntie Concepta was very, very fat. You couldn't see a chin. Great rounded folds were bursting through the buttons of her shirt and pants. She was nearly bald. The remaining wisps of hair were dyed blond. James wasn't fond of the smell of her. If smoking was so bad for you, how could she have lived so long? She always had a cigarette in the side of her mouth with smoke snaking up towards her closed left eye.

From the minute James stepped out of his mother's car on 20 December every year, to spend his Christmas holidays with Auntie Concepta, he had to do nearly everything for her.

'I'm out of breath James,' she said, sitting in the armchair by the stove with her huge round feet on a stool, 'make me tea. And bring me the *Racing Post* there boy. And then you can sweep the floor. And give the windows a little wash. And hurry up about it. The dogs need to be fed.'

James noticed that she got all her energy back when they were at the racetrack. It was like a miracle. She could run between the bookies' stalls shouting and bargaining as she laid bets on whichever of her dogs she had fed Red Bull to that morning. She laughed and swore and rushed down to the railing to watch the race. She cheered when her dogs got ahead. When they fell behind she shouted, 'Go on mongrel, or I'll break your legs.'

When a dog she had bet on lost, she amused everyone around by shouting to the dog, 'Com'ere chop suey, come to Mamma.' The same joke every time. Except James worried that it wasn't as funny as everyone else seemed to think.

Doing lots of work wasn't a bother for James. It helped pass the time as he counted down the days until 2 January when his Mam would be back for him. He especially didn't mind feeding the dogs. He spent hours every day in the cold dark outhouses where they were kept. The sheds were divided with chain link fences into very small spaces each shared by two or three dogs. There were thirty-five dogs in total this year.

James put his own names on the ones she hadn't bothered to name yet.

The dogs that would be racing soon got a long walk every day with Jack Carter. He was a yellow-skinned old man with a grubby red baseball cap. He never spoke to James. He just gave a nod for hello and a nod for goodbye. He was Auntie Concepta's trainer.

Most of the dogs never got out of the kennels because they were not in training. Some were too young. Others were bitches that had won prizes and Auntie Concepta was getting more pups from them. They looked at James with sad dark eyes, ears half-cocked and heads to one side, waiting for any kind word he might throw them. Talking to the dogs helped him stop worrying. James's biggest worry was that his Mum and Dad would have an accident on their skiing holiday and leave him here forever.

Leaving him with Auntie Concepta for Christmas was his Dad's idea. Dad's ideas always struck like lightning. Dad always thought they were brilliant even when they weren't. And his brainwaves gave him so much energy that he couldn't see how anything could go wrong.

His Dad thought it was great fun for James being here. Once, Dad's friend Cathal asked, 'But wouldn't James rather be with you guys for Christmas?'

'James,' Dad said, 'are you having me on! Concepta is gas craic. A real character. Everyone in racing has a story about

Concepta. James gets on with her like a house on fire. And there's nothing better for a lad than to spend time in the countryside. Give him a bit of independence. A sense of the wonder of nature – all the stuff we grew up with.'

Though he wasn't sure how a house on fire would be a good thing to get on with, James didn't complain. Maybe his parents needed a little time alone every year. They were always much nicer to each other when they came back. And Christmas was the only time they could both get off work.

His Mam wasn't so sure about it. She always cried as she drove off.

'James!' Concepta would say, rolling her eyes in disapproval as soon as Mam had gone, 'that's more like a sissy's name. I'll make a Jimmy out of you yet lad.'

❄ ♥ ❄

James was ten now. He didn't believe Auntie Concepta anymore. Every year he would ask her about the dogs that were missing from last Christmas. But this time he didn't believe they all had died of old age like she said. They wouldn't even have been four yet. And he knew they couldn't have been sold as pets. Every time he asked if he could take one home his Dad said that people didn't take such large scared dogs as pets – it would have been cruel to keep them in a city garden. Dad mustn't have known how small Auntie

Concepta's kennels were. A back garden would be like a dream place to these dogs.

Counting the days to New Year could sometimes be a slow process if he allowed himself to think about the dogs. So, most years, he tried not to think too much about them. But this year he couldn't help himself. His favourite pup from two years back would soon be running. He had grown from a pudgy ball of black into a very sleek, muscular athlete. It never occurred to James that Slate would be anything other than a champion. Slate would be the fastest dog that ever ran. James just knew it.

When Concepta told James they were bringing Slate to a coursing trial James was happy enough to go with them. They loaded the Hiace van. Jack sat in the front with Concepta. James sat in the back with two dogs. When the bumpy ride ended they were in a field he didn't know. It was only four o'clock but it was nearly dark already. There were a small number of people standing around complaining about how cold it was.

James didn't like watching coursing trials because he felt sorry for the hare. So he didn't watch until Slate was taken out. He had to watch this. Slate's competition was tall and beautiful. She glanced at James with kind eyes. But she was definitely not as beautiful as Slate. Concepta slapped the other owner on the back and shouted, 'Is that little bitch the best you've got? My hound will leave her standing!'

A short man with a walrus moustache pulled a potato sack from his truck. He untied it and let a hare out. It stood confused for a few seconds, looking all around. Both dogs caught sight of it and stiffened. Slate's tail curled. His muscles rippled. He was like a different animal. The hare realised the danger and darted off. Concepta released Slate slightly ahead of the whistle as though Slate needed to cheat.

'Go on you good thing,' shouted Concepta.

Slate tore off like the wind. It looked like his feet barely touched the ground in his doubled up motion. James was confused. He always felt sorry for the hare. But he couldn't help cheering for Slate, wanting him to get to the hare and turn it around. He was staring so hard at Slate, wishing him on, that he didn't even see where the hare or the other dog was. Concepta's string of curses woke him up though. The other dog was three full lengths ahead of Slate. And the hare was safely ahead of her, about to make its way to freedom through the far hedge.

'The black lad is a dud,' he heard someone mutter.

He didn't mind. Slate was still a beauty even if he wasn't actually the fastest dog that ever lived. James went to fetch him and gave him a good pat down just to console him. 'You're still the best dog in the world, old boy,' he said.

As he was getting the other dog from the van for the next trial he overheard a shabby looking man in a brown shop coat say to his wife, 'Will we take that black dog off Cepta?'

'Now Michael, we agreed, we can't take any more off her,' said the wife, a small woman with a kind face.

'But he's a grand dog and he might have just had a bad day. You know she never gives them a second chance. She's so severe on her dogs. Gives us all a bad name.'

'I know love but we can't take any more because …' she turned and noticed James near them and just smiled at him. She said loudly, 'Good little man James. Down with your Auntie for Christmas again? Aren't you a great fellow to take care of your Auntie like that when other young fellas are off playing PlayStations and demanding all kinds of yokes from their parents. Here take this.'

She gave him a tenner. He knew there was no point in trying to give it back. The dog people were always generous to other people. Nor could he tell them how much he would love to be off playing a PlayStation and getting nice things from his parents for Christmas, like he did before his Dad had this great idea.

He hugged Slate all the way back in the van. The yard was black when they arrived. Jack Carter opened the back to let him and the dogs out.

James was leading both dogs back to their kennels when Concepta's big hairy hand grabbed Slate's lead from him. 'Here, I'll take him, you take the other one back to her kennel.'

'Where are you taking him?' asked James.

'Don't concern yourself about that now like a good lad,' she said.

When James came back from putting Lady in the kennels, he heard whimpering from down the yard. He followed the sound and found Slate tied to a milk churn. He was shivering in the freezing night with the sweat not yet properly dried from him. James didn't know why he wasn't back inside with the others. But the sick feeling he had got worse when he saw Concepta shuffling across the yard towards him.

'Would you take your jacket off the bloody hound you soft eejit,' she laughed, 'he won't be needing it.'

As she stepped closer, James was the one who started sweating. Hanging from her heavy arm was the red hatchet that she used to break sticks that were too long for the range.

James suddenly heard himself pleading: 'Auntie, I was meaning to ask you earlier, can I have this old dog? I'll get him out of your way so he won't make you so angry. I want him for my Christmas present.'

She stopped to laugh loud and hearty. 'You might as well learn now, there's no room for pity in this business boy. A dog never disgraces Concepta more than once. You have to be cruel to be kind.' She was tapping the back of the axe on her other hand and James had no doubt left about what she intended to do.

Just then her mobile rang. She said, 'Where is that blasted

gadget?' as she rooted around in her apron pocket. She put the axe on the ground. She eventually got the phone out and said, 'Hello? Hello? Is that you Jack?'

'What? Come out for a drink? Sure Jaysus why wouldn't I. You'll come over to collect me then? Grand, grand that's the finest.'

She turned to James and said, 'I'll sort this out later. You go inside and mind the house.'

Luckily she didn't notice that the hatchet was gone. It was in James's hand. She was distracted and shuffled back into the house. A few minutes later she was back out with her pink overcoat on. She looked down the yard and called, 'Come on in here now lad and you can have a fig roll after you've washed them dishes.'

James had already used the hatchet to cut the baler twine leash as he wasn't able to undo the knot. He was hiding amongst the trees at the back of the yard whispering to Slate to be quiet.

When he didn't answer, she started walking down towards the churn, muttering, 'Useless spoiled brats these days, they'd want you to do everything for them.'

Then the car lights came down the lane. She forgot James and Slate for the time being. Carter carted her large form away.

James led Slate inside the house because he couldn't let go of him in case he ran off. Before James got his jacket and

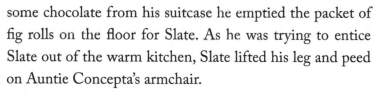

some chocolate from his suitcase he emptied the packet of fig rolls on the floor for Slate. As he was trying to entice Slate out of the warm kitchen, Slate lifted his leg and peed on Auntie Concepta's armchair.

'Come on boy,' said James, 'we've got a long mission. All the way back to Dublin. It could be twenty miles or maybe a hundred. I don't really know to be honest. And I don't really know the way. But we won't get there by standing here. I'm certain of that.'

Slate thought he was out for his training walk and he was very eager, pulling James along. The road was dark and eerie but it didn't frighten James very much because he kept telling himself that Slate would defend him against anything that might bother him.

The first thing that came along was a car. He saw the headlights from afar. But it didn't slow down as it got near. He had to jump into the hedge, pulling Slate with him. It was then he realised that they were invisible: the jet-black dog and the boy with the black coat. Every time he saw lights approaching after that he made sure he and Slate were already safely tucked in under a hedge or in a gateway to a field before the car got near.

James became very tired and Slate must have been tired too because he wasn't pulling so hard. But they kept walking because James really had no other plan. Every crossroads they came to, he made a guess. He ignored noises from the hedges. He had to tug really hard to stop Slate running off chasing things that he couldn't see. It might have been a few hours later when he started to feel sure he was back on the same road he had been on before. There was a bungalow that looked the same. And a round, stone gatepost. He was exhausted and he couldn't keep thoughts of sleep out of his eyes anymore. He went into a field and sat down by a large tree trunk. Slate knew what was on his mind and sat next to him. Then James pulled up the hood of his coat and curled up on the ground. Slate curled up next to him.

Later in the night there were lots of cars moving on that road. Some of them were racing and had flashing blue lights. But James and Slate slept through it all. James only woke when he felt long, warm breaths on his face. When he looked up, the overweight cow that was inspecting him got a bigger fright than he did, and darted off as Slate jumped up and barked.

They started off again. James was hungry and cold, but he was not going back. He patted Slate. 'At least we'll be able to see where we are going in the daylight, boy,' he said, 'so I promise we won't go around in circles.'

He was plodding along. His feet were very sore and damp. He was trying to think how you could work out directions from the sun. He had made a note of where it had risen. He knew that was to the east. But the road kept twisting this way and that so that he lost all sense. When he heard a car

approaching, he pulled Slate into the hedge as on the night before. But he forgot that they weren't invisible anymore. The car skidded on the chippings as it came to a halt.

He looked again. He couldn't believe it. It was his Mam's car. Mam and Dad left both front doors open as they ran out of the car to him. They were competing to lift him up. They were blubbering so much they weren't able to talk. And it took them a while to realise the reason they weren't able to lift him was because Slate was so heavy.

When his Dad opened James's jacket and saw the way he had the baler twine of Slate's lead tied around his belly, he said, 'Well I'll be! That's some knot you have tied there son.'

His Mam took out a scissors from her purse but James wouldn't let her near the string that secured Slate to him. She said, 'But then just let me loosen it a bit hon, it's cutting into your tummy.'

When they put him and Slate in the back seat of the car he said, 'Sorry I spoilt your holiday. I don't see why they called you. Everything was under control.'

'Under control, eh?' said his Dad.

James thought he heard him giggling until his Mam looked at him again.

'Yes. But I don't want to go back to Aunt Concepta.'

'You needn't worry about that, love,' Mam said.

James couldn't think very straight so he repeated what

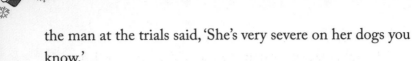

the man at the trials said, 'She's very severe on her dogs you know.'

He saw his parents glance at each other again. They looked confused but they didn't ask him what he meant.

'And I won't let you take Slate back there either,' he added. He meant that with his heart though he hadn't worked out how he would stop them.

If his parents were upset at their holiday being cut short, they didn't show it. They took him straight back home. It was Christmas Eve and he was where he wanted to be most of all.

In the morning he got the new games console he had asked for. He didn't even have to wait until 2 January to open it. But he didn't begin playing it straight away. He was still worried. Slate was in the kitchen and had pooed everywhere. That couldn't last. His Mam said, 'Why don't you go out in the garden and see what your lunatic of a Dad is up to now.'

James slid open the door. The back garden was in chaos. There were recliners, lawnmowers, and other stuff scattered in the rain. He got to the shed in time to meet the barbecue stand, his Dad's pride and joy, being flung out. All that was left in the shed was his Dad, a very big cushioned dog nest, and a silver bowl.

Dad said to him, 'I'm very sorry son. I get these mad notions sometimes. Next time I'm wrong, promise me you will just tell me?'

'OK,' said James.

'Though, mad as I might be,' he said with a cross look, 'I don't ever recall doing anything as mad as heading off into the wilds in the middle of the night with a hound tied to my belly and a hatchet in the lining of my coat!' He kept looking very seriously at James for a minute, and then he burst out laughing. James thought he would probably never understand his father.

James never asked about Auntie Concepta, but one day he heard his Dad talking on the phone in a very different tone. 'I'm ashamed I never took a closer look. The guards called the ISPCA in after James went walkabout. The kennels were too small and the conditions were all wrong. I suppose it all got beyond her. The bloody old rip. She's lost without the hounds; though, I believe she's getting into breeding snakes now, of all things. That should keep her amused.'

James hoped one of them would grow big enough to eat her, but that would probably take a long time.

MUMBLE CROFT'S CHRISTMAS ADVENTURE

JEAN FLITCROFT

Outside, a thick layer of snow lay across the fields like a new white carpet. Everything was perfectly still and even the birds at Croft Farm were silent for once.

Inside the farmhouse the fairy lights twinkled and the silver balls spun on the branches of the Christmas tree. A delicious smell of orange, spices and roasting turkey hung in the air.

In the kitchen, Mumble Croft was snuggled up in a tiny space beside the warm stove. His brothers and sisters were eating their dinner, slobbering and wolfing, arguing and pushing. Mumble just hoped there would be a little something left over for him.

Mumble had three brothers.

Rex was loud and bossy. He thought he was king of the pack. Herbert was serious and wise, perhaps a little too much for his own good. Max was tall and muscular, and a natural born leader.

Mumble also had three sisters.

Dora was perfect. She had the silkiest coat, the best teeth and knew she would win all the dog shows someday. Flora was adventurous, always climbing trees and eating plants that made her tummy ache. Sofia was the cleverest. She was gentle and shy but also a little smug.

And then there was Mumble.

Mumble was very different from the rest of the litter. He was much smaller than the other Labrador puppies, but his feet were twice as large so he was always falling over. He had a shiny pink nose while the others had black noses. His ears sat up as if he was always listening, whereas the others had ears that hung down by their head. His voice was small and he was still developing a proper bark. He was called Mumble because nobody could hear him and because nobody would listen to him anyway.

But Mumble could do one thing the other puppies couldn't.

He was the only one small enough to fit through the cat flap in the door to the kitchen. 'Here kitty, kitty,' the others would call and jeer at him as he disappeared out through the door every evening. But really, the others were very jealous.

While they were locked in the kitchen they knew that Mumble was out on his own having the most amazing night-time adventures.

His brothers and sisters pretended not to listen to his stories. Like the time that Mr Evans, the local baker, had given him a broken apple pie all for himself. He had tried to bring it home to share with the others, but the fresh apple and the buttery pastry was too much for the little pup to resist. Not surprising when he only got leftovers at home.

They pretended not to listen when he told them about the poacher he had chased off one day and the party that the rabbits and the birds had given him down in the lower field by the riverbank. He hadn't liked the nuts and carrots at the party, but had been far too polite to tell his friends that.

Now it was Christmas Eve, just ten minutes before midnight and Mumble heard the light tinkle of a bell outside. He actually had much sharper hearing than the others, although they would never admit it.

The others watched from the large foam cushion they shared in the centre of the kitchen as Mumble pushed the flap open and silently disappeared through it into the yard.

'Curiosity killed the cat,' Rex crowed.

Outside it was dark, but Mumble never minded the dark. His huge eyes, which had been much slower to open after his birth, were also much sharper than the others', although they would never admit that either.

Mumble heard the tinkle of the bell again, crystal clear in the cold night air. He ran towards it, tripping over his large feet and tumbling against the hooves of an enormous beast, who gave a loud snort of surprise.

Mumble stood up quickly, apologised for his clumsiness and stared. He had never seen anything like it before. The beast was about the size of a horse and he appeared to have big, furry tree branches strapped to his head. But most shocking of all was his large red nose that was glowing in the dark. Mumble touched his own pink nose thoughtfully with his paw, which is a hard thing for a pup to do. He was laughed at a lot for his pink nose.

Mumble took a step back and swallowed hard.

'I like your nose. It means that you can see very well in the dark.'

The horse with the branches on his head bent down low and smiled. He had huge yellow teeth.

'Thanks. A lot of my friends laugh at me because I'm different.'

Mumble hopped up and down on his huge paws. How wonderful, someone else like himself at last. 'Me too,' he said excitedly.

'Is there a song about you then?'

'I don't think so,' Mumble said doubtfully.

'Maybe there will be a story written about you some day.'

'I don't think so,' Mumble said again.

'Well I'll teach you my song if you like.'

And so, the horse with the tree branches on his head and the glowing red nose bent down and whispered it into the ear of the small dog with the big feet and the shiny pink nose.

When Mumble returned to the kitchen that night, he told his brothers and sisters all about his adventure. Rex roared with laughter. Herbert grinned knowingly. Max jeered wickedly. Dora giggled uncontrollably. Flora rolled on her back and laughed until she got a tummy ache and Sofia smiled sweetly in disbelief.

'A horse with a Christmas tree on his head?' they scoffed.

'No, no,' Mumble said.

'A Christmas tree bauble that got stuck on his nose!' they jeered.

'No, no …' Mumble shouted.

Then Mumble raised his chin and puffed up his chest and sang the song the horse with the tree branches on his head and the glowing red nose had taught him. He sang as loud as he could:

Rudolph, the red-nosed reindeer
had a very shiny nose.
And if you ever saw him,
you would even say it glows.

All of the other reindeer
used to laugh and call him names.
They never let poor Rudolph
join in any reindeer games.

Then one foggy Christmas Eve
Santa came to say:
'Rudolph with your nose so bright,
won't you guide my sleigh tonight?'

Then all the reindeer loved him
as they shouted out with glee,
Rudolph the red-nosed reindeer,
you'll go down in history!

It took two full verses for Rex, Herbert, Max, Dora, Flora and Sofia to stop laughing and begin to listen.

'Did you see Father Christmas too?' Sofia said jokingly.

Mumble nodded, his eyes sparkling.

'Did you mumble at him?' she asked smugly.

The others laughed.

'No. I told him all about you guys.'

Nobody said anything.

'I told him how Rex is top dog, Herbert is wise, Max is strong, Dora is beautiful, Flora is adventurous and Sofia is clever.'

'And what did Father Christmas say?' Herbert asked.

'Well, he said …' Mumble stopped embarrassed and mumbled for a bit.

'What did he say?' they all shouted together.

'Well, he said that I was good and kind and that that was the very best thing to be.'

His brothers and sisters stared at him, six pairs of eyes wide with amazement. And from that moment on, even though his voice was small and his feet too big and his ears stuck out and he had a pink nose, Mumble became the most important puppy at Croft Farm.

And you know, although he doesn't have his own song that we can sing, Mumble does have his own story now.

So he too can go down in his-story.

ONE-EURO SANTA

JOANNA BINCHY

(with help from her two little elves, Santiago, age 10 and May, age 6)

Once upon a time there was a Christmas tree in a lovely drawing room in a lovely house, whose owners had very good taste in ornaments and other things. The Christmas tree was covered in beautiful decorations. There were delicate coloured glass baubles that glinted in the fairy lights, clusters of frosted glittery bells that tinkled when the branch that they hung from shook, an antique cream and gold angel blowing a gilded trumpet, and lots and lots more attractive decorations.

But, low down, near the back, in the darkest, thickest part of the tree, lurked a cheap plastic one-euro Santa.

77

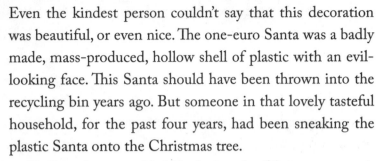

Even the kindest person couldn't say that this decoration was beautiful, or even nice. The one-euro Santa was a badly made, mass-produced, hollow shell of plastic with an evil-looking face. This Santa should have been thrown into the recycling bin years ago. But someone in that lovely tasteful household, for the past four years, had been sneaking the plastic Santa onto the Christmas tree.

Each and every midnight during the Christmas season, one-euro Santa and the antique cream and gold angel came to life. So it was that on the night before Christmas Eve, at midnight, plastic Santa was wriggling about trying to unhook his nylon string from the Christmas tree.

The antique angel, hanging high above him, couldn't help muttering, 'Ugly lump!' Although the angel tried not to, she couldn't help hating one-euro Santa; he was so vulgar and cheap.

Santa didn't hear her; someone was coming into the room. Santa peeped through the dark needles of the Christmas tree and squinted his crooked, blotchy eyes, and then suddenly he smiled.

It was *her*. The girl, who every year, for the past four years, had taken him out from his forgotten corner in the Christmas box and hidden him in the Christmas tree. Her name was Mary and she was seven years old. Santa waved at Mary; he knew it was against the rules to be seen alive by a human, but he didn't care.

Tonight she looked strange; she had some kind of tube in her arm and was pulling about what looked like a pole, with a bag on wheels. She shuffled over to the Christmas tree and parted the branches. Santa saw a pale face with dark-circled eyes. 'You're not supposed to be here. Me neither,' she whispered. 'Those stupid people who didn't bother to make you properly; I hope they all get coal for Christmas. See you as usual on Christmas morning!'

The next morning there was a commotion in the house. But Santa had to wait until midnight to ask the angel, who had a good view of everything that went on during the day, what the commotion was about.

At midnight one-euro Santa squirmed off his tree branch, while the antique angel flitted over to a Christmas card showing a snowy village scene. 'That poor child Mary,' said the angel, 'she became very ill; they had to take her to hospital. Such a pity, she shan't be here for Christmas.'

'Away for Christmas!' cried Santa. 'Away from her family! And away from me! Why my Christmas won't be at all right without her! I'm going to find her!'

Half an hour later, Santa was out in the cold night air. The outside world shocked Santa. It reminded him of himself: there were loads of ugly things everywhere; it wasn't at all like the snowy, pretty outside world in the Christmas cards.

The angel had told him to look for a huge concrete building with 'Hospital' written outside. The entire night

Santa trudged through the wet city. He walked and walked, but found no sign that said 'Hospital'. He was beginning to feel desperate; what would happen when dawn came and he was out on these cold, unfriendly streets? His cheap plastic body would become immobile again; he would be washed into a gutter and would never see Mary again.

And then suddenly, ahead, through the sinister orange light from the street lamps, loomed an enormous concrete building. In front of the building was a huge sign: Hospital.

Just as Santa ran forward, from a noisy open doorway, a large human being staggered. An enormous white training shoe came down towards one-euro Santa. And he remembered no more.

Mary awoke in her hospital bed just before dawn. She looked about her: on one side of her bed her mother was asleep in a chair. On the other side was an artificial Christmas tree. Underneath the Christmas tree was a shiny new toy ambulance driven by an extremely perfect blonde doll in a nurse's uniform; the real Santa Claus had brought presents in the night. Mary looked at the ambulance with its perfect driver and tried to like it. But the presents just weren't the same without her little friend, the plastic Santa, watching her from the darkest part of the Christmas tree.

And then something caught her eye. Something flat and dirty and plastic was hanging from one of the lower branches. Mary looked closer.

It was one-euro Santa! A very squashed and dirty one-euro Santa, but it *was* him. Mary leaned towards plastic Santa. There was a tiny sticking plaster across one of Santa's ugly eyes. 'I wonder how you got like that?' whispered Mary.

One-euro Santa squinted his one good eye down at the perfect nurse in her ambulance at the foot of the tree. 'Thanks for the lift,' he whispered to the nurse.

Mary rubbed one-euro Santa's squashed face. 'I'm glad you're here. Happy Christmas!'

With a great effort, Santa formed his flattened mouth into an awful smile. 'Happy Christmas to you too!'

REAL MAGIC

NEVILLE SEXTON

Eric used to be sad a lot. In fact, Eric remembers when he was sad nearly all of the time. He had always felt very different from the other boys and girls who ran and played everywhere around him. He couldn't do that you see … not like them. Sometimes his legs were funny and other times his tummy or head just didn't feel right. Often he was just too tired. Whatever the reason Eric felt unusual, lonely and unhappy – he just wanted to be like everyone else.

But all that changed on Christmas Eve when something quite amazing happened, and Eric knew he was never going to be sad again. And wait till you hear … it sounds made-up but it's real.

Like I said, it was Christmas Eve when Eric, all by himself, made this most incredible discovery. That day his legs and head were feeling weak … again! And so, while the heavy snow fell outside and a warm fire crackled in the fireplace, Eric was on the couch in his sitting room. Feeling bored and sleepy, and sad of course, he lay there staring upwards.

'I wish I was well enough to make a snowman,' he thought, as the white of the ceiling became a field of snow in his mind. With tears in his eyes he imagined crunching through the snow and chasing his friends. He heard the laughter and smiled as he imagined the fun he'd have. And that's precisely when the first strange thing happened: just then something cold and wet hit him on the head – it was a snowball.

'I'm dreaming,' Eric thought as he pulled the snowy lump from his hair. But this didn't feel like a dream. It felt real.

In that moment Eric realised he was no longer imagining the snow or the children. Instead, and to his great surprise, he was actually standing in a large snowy meadow with children running and giggling all around him. Before him stood a small girl.

'Hello,' the little girl said. 'You're Eric … wanna play?'

Eric looked at her and didn't quite know what to say. He was confused. He looked down at his feet and could hardly believe his eyes – he was standing. 'But –'

'I know,' interrupted the little girl, 'it's great here isn't it.'

'Here?' Eric asked, unsure. 'Where are we … Who are you … How do you know my name … How am I even standing?' he quizzed. He looked at his legs, both unusually straight and strong.

But of all the things that were racing through his mind – the hows, the wheres, the whos – the greatest feeling he had was, well … excitement.

'We can do anything we want here,' the little girl said smiling back at him. 'It's magic … see!' And just then she ran off through the snow. 'C'mon, catch me!' she shouted.

Eric's excitement took over. He put one foot in front of the other and before he knew it he was running. As he ran, however, he heard a strange noise. The sound, he realised, was laughter – his own. He'd never heard that before and he liked it.

'C'mon, you can do better than that,' the girl taunted. Then she did something very strange indeed. Just as Eric was about to catch her she began floating upwards, chuckling and laughing as she flew.

Without thinking Eric felt himself rising from the ground and up over the treetops. His belly gurgled with excitement as he floated up and down and round and round. He even knocked the snow off the highest tree branches as his outstretched arms skimmed over the forest below him.

Then, following the girl, he landed back on the ground.

'Is this a dream?' he asked her.

'No,' she said, again smiling. 'It's like a dream but you're actually awake in it. You decide what happens. Everything here is real too … just magic-real.'

'How did I get here?' Eric asked, suddenly afraid that he'd never find it again.

'That's easy,' the little girl whispered. 'All you have to do is think of me, think of this place, as you fall asleep. That's what I do. Now every time I go to sleep I wake up in this magic place and do everything I want.'

With that the little girl began to fade away and all Eric could see was white. But it wasn't snow – it was the ceiling. Eric took a deep breath as he woke up on the couch. He knew it had all been real.

That night Eric went to bed thinking of the wonderful place he'd found … and so, when he fell asleep, he woke up in the magic place again. He walked, he ran, he flew, he played … all night long.

In the morning Eric awoke with a smile. Not only because it was Christmas, but because he could feel that his legs were somehow stronger. With giddiness, he pulled off his blanket, climbed out of his bed and walked to the door. Then, for the first time in a long, long time, he made his way downstairs by himself and sat under the Christmas tree to open his presents.

Standing in the doorway Eric's Mum and Dad couldn't believe their eyes.

Eric turned to them and smiled, 'This is the best Christmas yet!'

And deep down Eric knew why: magic really was 'real'. So he kissed his parents and felt truly happy.

KANGAROO TED'S
CHRISTMAS ADVENTURE

DERMOT BOLGER (AGED 41¾) &
DIARMUID BOLGER (AGED 8½)

Up in the north where cold winds blow
    And Santa works with his elves,
Around the fire reindeer were gathered,
    Trying to warm themselves.

Then suddenly there came a shout
    From the oldest elf in charge:
'Look out, look out, there's a kangaroo about,
    In fact Kangaroo Ted is at large.'

Oh my goodness, what fuss and commotion,
    With toys knocked from their shelves:
Kangaroo Ted bounded with astounding motion,
    While being chased by all the elves.

'Get Kangaroo Ted under control.
    Quick, somebody put him in the sack,
Before he makes the bicycles roll
    And toy soldiers fall on their backs.'

Quickly they wrote a name and address
    And stuck it on his furry nose,
Then popped him in the sack with the rest,
    Where he bounced on a ballerina's toes.

Soon the other toys began to complain
    About Kangaroo Ted's bouncing about.
'Kangaroo Ted will drive us all insane,'
    All the rag-dolls started to shout.

Quickly they loaded up Santa's sleigh,
    Then, with one big almighty push,
The toys found themselves on their way
    As hooves churned the snow into slush.

Up, up they rose in the cold night air,
    Onwards through the wintry sky,
Until down below countries appeared
    And Santa grabbed his first toy.

'Is this Ireland?' shouted Kangaroo Ted,
    Urging on the reindeer herd,
As he bounded out from Santa's sack
    To climb along Santa's beard.

'Get off, get off,' Santa spluttered,
    'Your feet are hurting my nose.
We're only over Denmark,' he muttered,
    'Sit down or I'll bite off your toes.'

Kangaroo Ted refused to believe him,
    And climbed down the chimney as well,
Where he drank half of Santa's brandy,
    Then clambered up to ring Prancer's bell.

'Hurry up down there, Santa,' he called.
    'We haven't all night, you know,
You'll never find Ireland if you're drunk
    In all of this teeming snow.

In fact I think I should drive,
     I'd soon make these reindeer hop.'
'We'll chop you up for reindeer stew,'
     Warned Rudolph, 'if you don't stop.'

'Throw him in the sack,' begged Prancer,
     'Santa, he's driving us insane.'
'I've a better idea,' added Dancer,
     'Let's toss him overboard near Spain.'

'Now then, reindeer,' said Santa,
     'Kangaroo Ted's just a friendly chap,
Who's dying to meet his new playmate
     And snuggle up on his lap.'

So Santa flew quickly onward,
     Until he sighted land at Donegal,
He stopped in Ballybofey and Bundoran,
     In Naas, Navan, Nenagh and Naul.

He had mince pies in Macroom and Mountmellick,
     Fairy cakes in Feakle, Ferns and Foxford,
Guinness in Gort, Gorey and snowy Glencar,
     Hot whiskeys in White Gate and Wexford.

Over Dublin city he soon whirled
    By the light of a frosty moon,
Past decorations and streamers
    Hanging in every empty classroom.

'Are we here? Is this my new home?'
    Kangaroo Ted's head appeared,
Scattering presents over Drumcondra,
    As he swung out of Santa's beard.

'Kangaroo, I can't see where I'm going,
    Please stop covering my eyes,
Or else we'll crash in the playground
    And give the birds there a surprise.'

But Kangaroo Ted bounced so much
    That he fell over Santa's boot,
And might have been smashed to pieces
    If he had not grabbed a toy parachute.

Instead he floated over the houses
    As the reindeer landed with a thump,
To hold a sheet between their teeth
    For Ted to land in with a bump.

'Kangaroo Ted, you're finally here,'
  Said Santa: 'this is your new house,
And we'll wake every child within it
  Unless you go quiet as a mouse.'

So Kangaroo Ted crept down after Santa
  Leaving soot-marks across the room,
He watched Santa fill up the socks,
  Hoping his playmate would wake up soon.

He thought morning would never arrive,
  Until steps thundered down the stairs,
And excited children with sleep-filled eyes
  Appeared with smiles and tousled hair.

Kangaroo Ted thought his heart would burst
  As a boy hugged him to his chest
While back at the North Pole Santa slept
  Snoring happily in his old string vest.

FEENA'S CHRISTMAS TICKLES

PAULA LEYDEN

Feena waved goodbye to her Mum and wheeled herself down the path at the back of the garden and out through the small green gate into the woods. Her bright yellow wheelchair bumped over the stones as she headed for her favourite spot under the tallest oak tree.

The woods were Feena's special place. It was here in the summer that she listened to the sounds the leaves made. It was here she watched the peacock butterflies fluttering in the breeze and smelled the cool mossy earth. She imagined herself running over it and feeling it soft and furry underneath her feet.

Today was Christmas Day, there were no leaves on the oak tree and the air was cold. Feena had come out here to make a Christmas wish, a secret wish that nobody but her

knew about. She sat with her eyes closed tightly, but before she had a chance to wish anything she heard the branches shaking above her. She looked up, but there was nothing there. Then she heard it again, only this time she thought she heard a little voice.

That was impossible; nobody else was out here.

Feena closed her eyes again to try to make her wish, but then she heard the noise again. She grabbed her binoculars and pressed them hard against her eyes so she could look up into the tree. A tiny face peered at her through the glass and she took the binoculars away from her face as fast as she could.

A small, naughty face at the top of the oak tree? No, she must be imagining it. She looked again. Yes, the tiny grinning face was still there.

Feena held her breath and waited. The little creature, who wore a small black spider on her head, shouted down to her through a tiny megaphone, 'Hey Feena, come up here to see us. We've been watching you.'

Feena wasn't sure whether to answer. She was cross now.

'You silly galumph, can't you see I'm in a wheelchair?' she said.

'Oh, excuses, excuses! We'll bring you up ourselves if you can't manage it,' the odd little creature said.

'Will you look at the size of you,' Feena said. 'You're so small you could fit inside my ear. Why don't you come down here instead?'

Feena put down the binoculars and waited. Suddenly she felt a small whoosh of air and the little face, which now had a body, landed on her knee. Feena looked at her carefully. Yes that really was a spider on her head. It sat perfectly still, its bright eyes staring up at Feena.

'What is that spider doing sitting on your head?' Feena asked.

'Freddie? What do you think he's doing? He spins hats for me out of spider silk so my head is never cold. They are the best hats in the world. He's busy now spinning away, but you probably can't see. Would you like me to find a spider for your head?'

'No thank you,' Feena said. A warm hat was a nice idea, but she wasn't quite sure whether she wanted tickly spider legs wiggling around in her hair.

'OK,' the little creature said, 'you'll be sorry though when your ears turn into icicles. Speaking of ears, what makes you think I'd like to fit into yours? That's a very peculiar thing to say.'

'I just said that because you're too small to take me to the top of the tree. And I haven't climbed a tree since my legs got hurt, so I wouldn't be much help. What's your name anyway? And how do you know mine?' Feena asked.

'My name is Pod. And I'm not that small, you should see my cat if you want to see something really small. And I can hear, which is how I know your name. Your Mum has

a very loud voice … She's forever bellowing, "Feeeeeeena, Feeeeeena come inside now." Gives me a right headache. And there are other ways of getting to the top of a tree apart from climbing it. Use your imagination.'

Pod was a funny creature, but Feena was starting to like her. She was bossy all right, but Feena didn't mind that. And she didn't seem to care much about the fact that Feena was in a wheelchair. In fact, she seemed to like it. She was hopping around it, inspecting the boxes and buttons and hanging off the spokes of the umbrella which Feena always carried in case of a rain, snow or sunshine emergency. This was a different kind of emergency, though – the arrival of a small, grumpy creature with a spider on her head.

'This is cool. I wonder would they make one for me. Does it go fast?' Pod said.

'As fast as I want it to, which is very fast if I'm on a smooth road. To make one small enough for you would be very hard, it would have to be made by tiny hands so I can't help you there,' Feena said. 'And, since you're so full of ideas, what other ways are there for getting to the top of a tree?'

'Flying, leaping, somersaulting, swimming, kicking, ballooning, burping, hitching a ride, thinking, snorting, twirling …'

Pod sounded as if she would never stop, so Feena interrupted her. 'Kicking? That's just silly.'

'Oh no it's not. And you wouldn't be doing the kicking; you'd be the one being kicked. A good strong kick on your backside and up you'd go. Easy.'

Feena looked up at Pod who was hanging by one arm from the umbrella. 'That would be sore. And swimming, how do you swim up a tree?'

Pod jumped down from the umbrella and stopped in midair right in front of Feena's face.

'OK, swimming I just added in because I felt like it. But if it was very rainy and the whole world was flooded, then swimming would work.'

Feena decided not to ask about the other ways, they all sounded perfectly ridiculous.

'How do you stay like that, floating in the air without any wings?' she asked.

'Thinking is how I do it, I just think "up in the air" and that's what happens,' Pod said.

'Think yourself upside down then,' Feena said.

'When I feel like it I will. I don't do tricks, even though I can. I can do anything,' Pod said, 'even take you to the top of the tree. Then you can meet my cat, he's called Thunk.'

'Thunk? Is that because you think?' Feena asked.

'I suppose so … but really it's because that's the noise he makes when he runs down the stairs: thunk, thunk, thunk.'

Pod suddenly tumbled through the air and landed on Feena's lap.

'You see what happens when I stop thinking about staying in the air? Lucky you were there. Otherwise I might have hurt myself and it would be all your fault. So, have you decided yet? Are you coming up the tree? I haven't got all day to be hanging around waiting for you.'

'What if Mum comes looking for me to call me for my Christmas dinner?'

'Well, we'll hear her bellowing and then we'll drop you back into this fast, yellow wheelchair and she won't even know you've been away. Please.'

Feena looked at Pod. This was the first time she had asked nicely, and it would be fun to be at the top of her favourite tree. She may as well try.

'OK. But don't keep me there forever, I'd miss home if I was away too long,' she said.

Pod, with a delighted grin on her face, whispered in Feena's ear and gave a hard pull on her hair.

'Ow!' Feena said, but before she could complain, or pull Pod's hair back, she felt a fierce wind blowing and it seemed as if she was tumbling upwards through the air.

As quickly as it had started, the wind stopped. Feena found herself sitting on a small wooden ledge surrounded by hundreds of little creatures who looked just like Pod. And right in front of her sat a small, grey cat with bright purple eyes. She looked down and caught a glimpse of her empty wheelchair, far down below. She looked up again.

She was right at the very top of the oak tree and everyone was staring at her, even the cat called Thunk.

'Hello,' she whispered.

They all jumped.

'Sorry,' she said, a little louder this time. Then the twittering started. It sounded as if a thousand sparrows had arrived. She couldn't make out one word. Where was Pod?

'Here I am, you didn't think I'd bring you up here and then leave, did you? And what a noise you made when you landed. You nearly destroyed our house. That's not very good behaviour for a visitor.'

Pod sounded very cross as she stood there with her hands on her hips.

'How did I get here?' Feena asked. She felt a little worried now.

'What did I tell you? One of the ways you can get up a tree is by somersaulting through the air and that's exactly what you did. You're very good at it, for a learner.'

Feena suddenly felt an itchy, tingly kind of feeling on her legs. She had not felt that for a very long time, not since the accident three years ago. She stretched her arm out to scratch it and heard a chorus of small screams. Her hand stopped in midair and she looked down to see all the little creatures running up her legs.

'Don't worry Feena, they just want to see you. And touch you. They've never been this close to a giant human being

like you. Just sit still and don't breathe too hard otherwise they might fall off,' Pod said.

'Mum said to me that if I start feeling anything in my legs that's a good sign. My legs might start working again. I can feel their feet on me,' Feena said.

'Ah well,' said Pod, 'soon you won't be needing me to get you up the tree then.' She sounded disappointed. 'But you can come and visit any day, isn't that right Thunk?' She scratched Thunk's head as she spoke.

Suddenly Pod started shouting, 'Off now, leave her alone you wretched galoots. Go back to the house with your fidgety little legs.'

All the creatures jumped off Feena in a big cloud of floating hair and squeaky voices.

Feena felt her head drooping with tiredness and her eyes closing. She felt as if she was losing her balance. She woke up with a start as she heard her mother's voice, 'Feena, Feena, wake up. Look, aren't they pretty? Ladybirds arriving on Christmas Day, how peculiar.'

Feena was back in her wheelchair and her Mum was pointing to her legs. Feena looked down; her legs were covered in ladybirds, red ones and yellow ones. She looked up at her Mum, 'Mum I can feel their little feet, even through my tights. They're tickling me.'

Feena's Mum laughed, a big loud laugh – it was just the way she used to laugh before Feena's accident.

'Are you sure Feeny? You can feel them?' Feena's mother was hopping about with excitement as she spoke.

Feena smiled and looked up into the branches. She was absolutely sure she could hear another laugh up there, not as loud as her Mum's but still a laugh. High-pitched and a little bit wicked.

She looked down again at the hundreds of ladybirds. Her Christmas wish had come true before she had even had the time to make it.

THE MUCKY, RAGGY LITTLE RIBBON

TERRY PRONE

Two boxes. Two Christmas gifts, neatly wrapped, under the tree. They had different shapes. But the main difference between them was the ribbon.

One of the presents had a pink ribbon. It was nearly as broad as a baby's wrist. Because it was made of satin, it was shiny. Not only was it shiny, but it had a sparkly silver thread running through it. It glittered. When the lights on the Christmas tree went on, it really sparkled.

The pink sparkly ribbon crossed the parcel to form a big bow in the middle. The bow was perfect. Each loop was exactly the same length. The loose ends had all been curled.

They were like little pink springs. You'd want to touch them. You'd want to push the curls together gently and see if they would spring back when you let go of them.

Other gifts around the tree had different coloured ribbons on them. Some of them were dull red. Some of them were acid yellow. Some of them were deep orange. All of them were new. They were smooth. They were gorgeous.

Except for the ribbon around the second package, right beside the one with the pink ribbon. That ribbon was some kind of a colour. Some sort of a colour. But it would be hard to put a name on the colour for two reasons. First of all, the ribbon wasn't quite dirty, but it wasn't quite clean either. You'd love to stick it in the washing machine, except it wasn't the kind of thing you could put in the washing machine. It was too delicate. If you put it in with the clothes for washing, it would come out like a piece of twine, if it came out in one piece at all.

The ribbon was faded, too. That was the second factor making it difficult to work out what colour it was. Or, rather, what colour it had been when it first appeared.

You could almost see the pink ribbon beside it trying to get away from it. The pink ribbon was puffy and proud of itself. The ribbon around the other package was neither puffy nor proud. It looked like a poor relation. It looked kind of sad, as if it knew the pink ribbon was sneering at it, as if it knew the pink ribbon thought it was a mucky

103

little, raggy little string that should be ashamed to find itself under the Christmas tree.

Presents under the Christmas tree can't move, we all know that. The pink ribbon parcel couldn't actually push the other parcel to one side so that it was hidden away at the back. Maybe it was just that the presents settled a bit, like cornflakes in a box. Or maybe I opened the door so suddenly that I created a wind and the wind knocked over some of the presents.

I don't know the reason, but I do know that when I stood in front of the tree, I couldn't even see the package with the mucky little, raggy little string ribbon. Even when I went down on my hunkers I couldn't see it. I got into a complete panic. Not because it was a present to me. It wasn't. It was a present from me to my Dad. TO DAD FROM LISA WITH ALL MY LOVE FOR A HAPPY CHRISTMAS, I had printed on it. But now I couldn't see it at all.

I pushed the present with the pink ribbon aside and there it was, the parcel with the raggy ribbon around it. I lifted it up and put it right on top of the pink ribbon present. Now, putting it there was going to squash the pink ribbon a bit. And the pink ribbon present was addressed to me from my big sister. But I didn't care. I wanted the present with the mucky ribbon to be right where everybody could see it. In the best place, up on the top.

That's because I know what the ribbon used to look like.

The ribbon was white as snow, with a silver thread through it. My Mam tied it around a present for me when I was six. She made it so pretty that I didn't want to take the ribbon off. But I didn't want to take the ribbon off that Christmas, five years ago, for another reason. Mam was very sick. I knew she was very sick. I think I knew she was going to die, but I had this feeling that if I didn't do anything, if I didn't open my presents, I could stop time and stop her dying.

'Lisa, love,' Mam said to me, 'why are you not opening your present from me?'

I couldn't answer her. I didn't mean to cry, but I did. Mam was lying on the couch, and she reached out and pulled me over to her. She didn't say anything for a long time, and I couldn't say anything because I was crying. Tears were falling right down on the white ribbon with the silver thread running through it.

'Tell you what,' Mam said, when I quietened down a bit, 'open your present. But save the ribbon. Save the ribbon and wrap it around a present for your sister Maeve next year. And for your brother David the year after. And for your Auntie Mae the following year. And then for your Dad. Keep it until it gets mucky and raggy. Keep it as a little connection to me – and remember it's only one of thousands of little connections. That's what love is. A thousand little connections and things you refuse to forget.'

So each year since, I've tied the ribbon around a fresh

present and taken it back afterwards. The funny thing is that the person who gets it each year thinks it's much better than a new puffy pink ribbon. Tomorrow, Dad will be sad when he holds my present, but it will start him talking about Mam and that will make him happy again.

Christmas wouldn't feel right without my mucky, raggy little ribbon.

THE MAGIC BOOTS

GER GALLAGHER

Baakir was a seven-year-old boy who lived in a village in Africa. He lived with his mother and father and his little sister Yasmin, who was three. Baakir went to school every day and, because there wasn't very much else to do, he spent most afternoons playing football with his friends. Baakir was the most popular boy amongst his friends because he had a very special talent: he was the best footballer in the village. When his team won the school boys cup, Baakir was voted player of the year. He was presented with a pair of football boots that had come all the way from America and were signed by David Beckham. Baakir treasured the boots and after each match, he cleaned them and put them back inside the white box they had come in. He called them his

magic boots, because every time he put them on they made him play the most incredible football.

One day, Baakir's mother came into his bedroom and told him to pack as much as he could carry because they were going on a journey. Outside his window, Baakir saw smoke coming from the hills and heard the sound of gunshots in the distance. As his mother helped him pack, she told him that the rebels were fighting in the hills and that she was afraid they may come down to the village and harm them. Baakir's father had already left to help at the university where he worked. On the bus to the airport, Baakir's mother held Yasmin on her knee and explained to them that they were going on a long journey to a country called Ireland, where Aunt Florence was living. When the rebels stopped fighting, they could go back to their village again. Baakir didn't want to leave, but he knew that if the rebels came down from the hills, his village would not be a safe place to be. He thought of what he had packed and was suddenly filled with panic when he realised he had left his magic boots in the white box on the floor of his bedroom.

'Mama,' he cried, jumping up from his seat. 'We must go back. I left my magic boots behind.'

His mother put her hand on his arm and pulled him down beside her. 'We can't go back now. It's too dangerous.'

Baakir sat down quietly and tried not to cry.

At the airport, his mother received a call from his

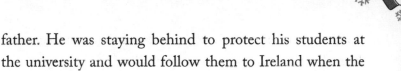

father. He was staying behind to protect his students at the university and would follow them to Ireland when the fighting stopped.

Baakir had always dreamed of going on an aeroplane, but as they climbed high into the clouds he didn't feel at all excited because he was leaving his father and his magic boots behind.

Ireland was very different from Africa. It was November and Baakir had never felt so cold in all his life. No matter how many clothes he wore, the cold crept inside his bones and made him shiver. They moved into a house beside his Aunt Florence and she showed them around the neighbourhood. There was a playground nearby and some shops and a boys school where Baakir would go. Yasmin was too young for school and Baakir envied her because she could stay at home with his mother. At school he didn't talk to any of the other boys because he couldn't understand their accents. They spoke English differently to the way Mr Kabila, his English teacher, had taught him. For the first two weeks at school, Baakir sat on his own at lunch time and didn't make any friends because nobody seemed to know what he was saying. He was lonely and miserable and wanted more than anything to be back in his village with his friends. His mother tried to cheer him up: 'You have joined the football team. When they see how well you play every boy in school will want to be your friend.'

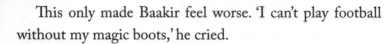

This only made Baakir feel worse. 'I can't play football without my magic boots,' he cried.

'But you were always a great footballer, even before you got the boots,' his mother exclaimed.

Baakir shook his head. 'I just know that I won't ever be able to score a goal again without them.'

On Saturday morning Baakir walked up to the football pitch for his first match. He had borrowed a pair of football boots from Aunt Florence's next-door neighbour, but they felt all wrong on his feet. He wished his mother hadn't told the coach what a good player he was, she just didn't understand; without his boots, Baakir had lost his magic. It was a pretty good match, Baakir played well and the teams drew nil–all, but he knew that if he had worn the magic boots, he would have easily scored a goal.

The same thing happened the following Saturday. Baakir played well, but when it came to striking, he kicked the ball wide, missing his chance to score for the team.

In school, the teacher told the boys they could write their Christmas letters to Santa.

Baakir thought about all the toys and games that the kids in his class had: laptops, PlayStations, trampolines, electric scooters – things that he and his pals in Africa had only ever dreamed of having. But the only thing Baakir wanted for Christmas was to see his father. He had given up hope of ever getting the magic boots from his house in Africa, but

he hadn't given up hope of seeing his father again. Baakir's mother cried a lot every evening. He could hear her through the walls of his bedroom. He knew she was upset because his father hadn't called them in weeks and they couldn't get through to his mobile phone.

As the weeks went by, Baakir played great football, but he still didn't manage to score any goals. He thought of his friends in Africa and how they wouldn't believe it if they heard that their best player had stopped scoring goals.

The weather became colder and all the kids in his class began to get excited about Christmas. Baakir's English had improved and it was easier for him to understand their accents. They all talked about what they were getting from Santa, but when they asked Baakir what he was getting, he just shrugged his shoulders. It would have sounded foolish to say that all he wanted for Christmas was to see his father again.

Aunt Florence told Baakir that if he really wanted something he should write it down on a piece of paper everyday and wish for it with all his heart. Every morning before he went to school, Baakir wrote 'My father' on a piece of paper and held it to his forehead and wished as hard as he could. But as Christmas Day approached, it looked as if his wish would not be granted. Baakir's mother continued to pace the floor every night waiting for her husband to ring, but no call came. On Christmas Eve, Baakir's mother was

111

upstairs bathing Yasmin while Baakir sat at the living-room window staring out into the darkness. He was thinking to himself about what a terrible Christmas it was going to be, when two amazing things happened.

The first thing was that it began to snow. Baakir had never seen snow before and he looked out in wonder at the white flakes as they swirled down through the darkness. He ran outside, stood in the front garden and felt the cold snowflakes on his face. It was like stepping into a snow globe. Baakir threw his head back and looked up as the white, cottony snow fell silently around him. The second amazing thing happened a few seconds later. Baakir was frozen to the spot when he saw a man in a long, dark coat walking towards his house. He wiped the snowflakes from his eyelashes and blinked a few times to make sure he wasn't dreaming because, as the man got closer, Baakir realised it was his father.

Baakir's father dropped his suitcase on the snow-covered grass and they hugged each other tightly. Baakir's mother let out a loud scream as she came downstairs and saw her husband standing at the door. Inside the warm kitchen, Baakir's mother made coffee while his father told them how he had flown on three aeroplanes to get to his family for Christmas. They sat up for a long time and his father talked about people from their village and where they had gone. Baakir began to get tired and his mother told him to go to bed or Santa wouldn't come to the house. His father came to kiss him goodnight and Baakir realised that, even though he was a long way from home, he was happier than he had ever been before. It was Christmas and his family were back together again and that was the best gift he could ever have wished for. His father sat on the edge of the bed and opened the bag he was holding. 'You know, I went back to the village one night when the rebels were sleeping and I crept into our house.'

Baakir began to shake with excitement as his father took the white box out of the bag.

'And I found these, in the exact place where you had left them.'

He took the lid off the box and sitting inside were the magic boots. Baakir opened his mouth to say something, but he was lost for words.

His father kissed him. 'Now, you must get some sleep. We'll have lots of time to talk tomorrow.'

It was the best Christmas ever. Baakir had his father, his magic boots, snow and of course his presents from Santa. When football started up again after the Christmas holidays, Baakir's team won two–nil, and guess who scored the goals?

Baakir never returned to Africa. He still lives in Ireland. In school, the boys have given him a new name – Baakir Beckham – because he is the best footballer they have ever had on their team.

CHRISTMAS BY EMAIL

DAN BOYD

19 December

Dear Brooke,

It was great to hear from you yesterday. I just love being pen pals – especially with email. I can't imagine what it would have been like all those years ago when you had to wait for days for the postman, like our Mums had to do. You're so lucky to live in sunny Australia. It's hard to imagine Christmas in summer. Then again, I can't imagine a summer as nice as the ones you get. I would give anything to be there now – really sounds fab.

Someday …
Aisling

20 December

Hi Brooke,

I can't believe you're taking surfing lessons! That is really cool. I love the photo you sent me of Santa. He looks really funny in his Bermuda shorts!

Dad just arrived with even more decorations, so I know what I'll be doing all day … If you see a slight glow in the northwest – that's our house!

The 'Carols by Candlelight' concert you're practising for sounds great. I bet it will be beautiful. Would probably rain on us if we tried it here, or worse still my Dad would join in and embarrass me to death.

Talk soon,
Aisling

21 December

Brooke,

No believe me; my Dad's singing is that bad. If he were busking on Grafton Street, people would pay him … to stop.

My arms are killing me from carrying in all the groceries. I think Mum bought half the shop – our fridge is bulging now. Well has your Mum decided on what you're doing for Christmas dinner? Barbecue in the back garden or picnic on the beach – tough call, either one sounds amazing! I'd trade a turkey dinner for a sambo on the beach any day.

You are so lucky not to have any pesky brothers or sisters. I could have killed Connor this morning. He was using glue to make a Christmas card and somehow ended up gluing it to my hair! Don't ask me how. He ripped the card from my head and stormed off after I yelled at him. He deserves to be upset – brothers!

Gotto go wash my hair … again!

Aisling

24 December

Brooke,

I've been crazy busy getting ready for Christmas. Yesterday we all went into town. Dublin was magical; there was a real buzz about the place. Grafton Street has these new lights – well they're actually giant chandeliers – they look amazing! The buskers and choirs were out in force getting everyone in the spirit. At one stage Dad joined in. I was mortified at first but then figured what the heck and joined in as well! We had so much fun. In fact that's what we did most of the day – laughed. We actually laughed more than we shopped, which is saying a lot.

We had dinner in town before taking in the giant Christmas tree made of balls in the middle of O'Connell Street. It is so cool. I'll be sure to send photos of it.

I had the best day ever. Just before going to bed Connor gave me the card he made. It was bent up and torn a little. It even still had a few of my hairs stuck to it! But it was the best card a big sister could ever get. On the front he had drawn a picture of our family and on the inside it said, 'world's greatest family'. I couldn't have said it better myself!

We may not have the sun or the beach or the barbecue but I've come to realise what we do have is ... well paradise! And I wouldn't change anything!

Happy Christmas,

Aisling ☺

ÁINE'S STAR

FIONA CASSIDY

It was Christmas Eve and a little girl wearing pink pyjamas who had brown curly hair and a button nose was looking up at the sky from her bedroom window. She was searching for the stars that were usually there. She also wanted to see if she could spot Santa, as she needed to tell him that she lived in a new house. Áine liked stars. She especially liked the star song that Mammy sang to help her fall asleep.

Twinkle Sparkle Áine's Star
What a special girl you are
Up above the sky at night
Your little friend shines so bright
Twinkle Sparkle Áine's Star
Go to sleep. Dreams aren't far.

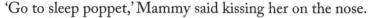

'Go to sleep poppet,' Mammy said kissing her on the nose.

'But Mammy I won't be able to sleep,' Áine said. 'I'm too worried to sleep.'

'Worried?' Mammy asked, puzzled.

'Yes Mammy. How is Santa ever going to find me? He'll go to our old house and leave my baby elephant there.'

Mammy cuddled her close. 'Of course Santa will find you. Santa is very clever. He knows everything.'

Áine wasn't sure. She thought that Santa might be too busy delivering presents all around the world to wonder where she had gone.

Mammy stroked her hair and left the room.

Áine knelt on her bed, moved the curtain and looked out at the night sky. It was very dark.

Her big sister Úna came to kiss her goodnight.

'What's wrong baby?' she asked, cuddling her.

'Santa's not coming,' Áine said glumly.

'Of course Santa will come,' Úna said. 'The little elephant you want is looking forward to seeing you.'

Áine smiled sadly. She thought of the soft, fluffy grey elephant she had seen in the toyshop window. It would still be there after Christmas because Santa wouldn't be able to find his way to her house.

Áine cuddled into her big sister and sighed.

'Would it help if I told you a story?' Úna asked.

'OK,' Áine said feeling a bit happier.

119

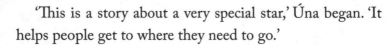

'This is a story about a very special star,' Úna began. 'It helps people get to where they need to go.'

'Is it my star?' Áine asked.

'It could be,' Úna answered.

'Once upon a time there were three men who lived in a land far, far away. These men were told about the birth of a very special baby boy and because they were very kind they wanted to bring the new baby some gifts.'

'Did the baby want an elephant?' Áine asked suddenly.

'The baby was too small for an elephant,' Úna said. 'I think he just wanted a nice blanket and maybe some milk.'

'Did the baby not have a blanket and milk?' Áine was thinking about her own baby sister who had so many toys and clothes and blankets that they nearly touched the sky.

'The baby's mammy and daddy were very poor,' Úna explained. 'The baby was born in a stable with cows and donkeys for friends.'

'But no elephants,' Áine said.

'No elephants,' Úna sighed. 'The three men tried to find the baby but they got lost and were very sad. They asked lots of people if they knew where the baby lived but nobody could help them. They stopped to rest and fell asleep under a tree. When they woke up they had to cover their eyes because the biggest, brightest star they had ever seen was shining down on them.'

'My star,' Áine shouted.

'Yes it was your star,' Úna said. 'They saw that the star was moving so they decided to follow it. The light from the star was very bright and it led them through strange towns and villages until it stopped outside an inn. While they were there they asked about the new baby. To their surprise the innkeeper knew all about him and told them that he was sleeping nearby.

'When they went outside they saw that their star had gone but then they heard a baby crying.'

'The special baby,' Áine said.

'He was a very important baby. He was king of the world.'

'Wow,' Áine said.

Úna moved the curtain and looked outside. 'Look Áine,' she cried. 'Look at the star shining above us. That's the magic star that will guide Santa to our house. That's your star.'

Áine climbed into Úna's arms and looked at the sky and there, sure enough, was the brightest star she had ever seen.

She smiled sleepily and, as she lay down and closed her eyes, she thought about the baby king. She could hear sleigh bells in the distance. She also thought she heard a baby elephant trumpeting, and guess what? In the morning she knew she had, as there, at the end of her bed, was the fluffy elephant she had asked Santa for.

Áine thought about her special star.

'Happy Christmas little friend,' she whispered.

HOME SWEET HOME

FIACHRA SHERIDAN

Home sweet home for Jah the Gick Na was a crack under the railway bridge in Ballybough. It was beautiful in the summer but the winter cold gave the black stones a permanent icy layer that made sleeping impossible. Every morning before breakfast Jah would go to Connolly Station for a few cigarettes. Sweet Afton were his favourite because they had no filters. Swallowing filters gave him awful indigestion. He couldn't believe Connolly was deserted; there wasn't a paying customer in sight. Christmas, he thought, it must be Christmas, the worst day of the year for a scavenging pigeon.

Most pigeon lofts were built outside, but Bobby's was on top of the wardrobe in his bedroom. It was the only loft in Ballybough that had never seen a pigeon. Christmas morning was going to change all that. Bobby's eight-year-old brain had it all worked out. He would exercise his pigeon twice a day, massage him and do whatever it took to have a champion racer. He had yet to get a firm grip on Santa's understanding of how Christmas presents work:

Rule number thirty-three: Christmas presents should not become a burden on the parents of said child.

Bobby's Dad said pigeon food cost a fortune and they could hardly afford to put food in their own mouths. Bobby sneaked downstairs at twenty past seven. He looked around for the cardboard box, the one he described to Santa in the letter, with holes all around the side so the pigeon could breathe. It was nowhere to be seen. There was a letter on the floor in front of the smouldering fire:

I'm very sorry Bobby, but the pigeons didn't breed due to the cold weather in the North Pole this year.
Enjoy Christmas,
Santa

❄ ♥ ❄

Jah found it difficult to land with one leg, but he was used to it. He would turn sideways just before landing to even out the impact. He was a master scavenger, much better than his younger rivals. He never let any of them follow him to his secret feeding points. He knew the old lady in Richmond Cottages threw crispy crumbs out after Mass every morning. The Holy Grail of feeding points was to find someone foolish enough to throw out their crusts. Jah lost his leg in a fight over a crust: the leg had held the orange loop of the best racing pigeon in Dublin.

If Santa couldn't breed a pigeon then Bobby would snare one. He would use black thread to camouflage it against the concrete. Eight-inch diameter loop at one end, fast fingers at the other end and crusts all around the inside of the circle. There were thousands of pigeons in the derelict houses around Ballybough, thought Bobby, and any one of them could be good enough to be a champion.

Just as a group of potential racers was about to enter the catch zone, a huge seagull swooped down and grabbed at the bread, frightening all the pigeons away. When the seagull left, Jah saw his window of opportunity. He landed sideways right in the middle of the circle and quickly saw what was on offer. Top crusts! Bobby snapped the thread and Jah dropped the bread. He managed to rise four feet in the air before Bobby pulled him in. Bobby slid his hand underneath the pigeon and tried to grip the legs between his fingers. He didn't need to look down to realise there was one missing. Jah looked down and saw the pile of crusts at Bobby's feet. Bobby took off the snare, raised his hand in the air and released the pressure, expecting the pigeon to fly up into the sky.

There are more crusts where they came from, Jah thought to himself. He balanced on Bobby's hand and flapped his wings.

'I'm looking for a racer,' said Bobby as he threw his hand up in the air a second time. Jah inhaled as deeply as he could and took off down the road, doing a U-turn at the bridge, before speeding back to Bobby in record time. He felt like he was having a heart attack, but Bobby was seriously impressed with his speed and the fact that he landed on his shoulder. Jah was so out of breath he didn't know where he had crashed. His eyes were blurry and his head was fuzzy but he tried not to show it. 'You're a serious racer,' said Bobby.

Drink, thought Jah, I need a drink.

❄ ♥ ❄

'Santa really is magic,' said Bobby over Christmas dinner.

'Did you love your presents?' asked his Mam.

125

'Every one of them, especially my racer.'

'Racer?' asked his Dad suspiciously.

'Jah the racer, Santa left the box in my room.'

'Santa didn't bring you a pigeon,' said his Dad.

Dinner had to be put on hold as Bobby got up to prove his father wrong. He carried Jah slowly down the stairs. 'Don't dare put that near the table,' said his Mam when she saw the holey box. Bobby placed it on the floor and opened the lid. He put his hand in and expected Jah to jump up. He couldn't: three crusts in two hours after a warm sudsy bath was making movement impossible. Bobby held up the glistening bird.

'Coo, coo coo,' said Jah.

'Home sweet home,' laughed Bobby as he kissed him on the beak.

I KNOW WHAT
I WANT FOR CHRISTMAS

DECLAN FRY

'I know what I want for Christmas!' said Billy Brown excitedly as he turned to face his little brother.

'What?' asked Jimmy, his eyes wide open in wonder and delight.

'A brand new racing bike! With twenty, or thirty or maybe even fifty gears!'

'That sounds cool. I want one of those too!' said Jimmy, even though he had never thought about a racing bike before that moment and he didn't have the slightest idea what a gear was.

But he adored his big brother.

And if you had been hiding in their room that night

listening to the two brothers talking as they lay wide awake in that double bed, you might have imagined that Christmas was only weeks away.

But you would have been wrong.

It was only May.

Anyway, poor little Jimmy Brown was only fooling himself if he thought that Santa Claus was going to bring him something like a new racing bike.

It's not that Santa hadn't been good to him over the past few years, he most certainly had.

There was the board game that he had wanted and the brand new football boots last year. And the year before that he got a rugby ball, a new *Beano* annual and a selection box!

But he never did quite as well as Billy.

It was Billy who got the skateboard, Billy who got the new tennis racket and, of course, Billy who got the scooter.

Poor little Jimmy Brown.

He just had to wait his turn and one day all those things would be his. It's just that when he did get them, they wouldn't be new.

Mrs Brown was just hanging the last of the shirts on the line when she heard the crash. She dropped the shirt immediately and ran towards the house, all the time hoping that what

sounded like the milk jug smashing on the kitchen floor tiles was exactly that.

As long as nobody was hurt. That was the most important thing.

But there was nobody in the kitchen, or the utility room, or, as far as she could tell, out in the hall. In fact everything looked just as she had left it. No sign of any damage at all.

It was then that she noticed the sitting-room door. It was ajar and it shouldn't have been. If she had told them once she had told them a thousand times ...

She felt sure, as she walked slowly down the hall, that she could hear whispering, but as she pushed the door open all that greeted her was silence. Silence – and the sight of her two sons standing in a pool of smithereens with Jimmy holding what remained of her favourite lamp.

'What have you done?' said Mrs Brown when she finally managed to speak. 'You shouldn't even be in here. I told you that!'

'It wasn't me, it was his idea!' said Billy straight away. 'He told me you wouldn't mind.'

'I didn't Mam, I didn't,' little Jimmy protested.

But his mother wasn't listening. She was far too upset.

Time went by as it always does and Mrs Brown didn't stay

angry forever. In fact, her anger probably only lasted about two days. She loved her boys thousands of times more than any lamp and they knew that.

By November, that afternoon in May and the broken lamp were both long forgotten as Billy and Jimmy Brown sat down to write their letters to Santa. Two brand new racing bikes and two shiny new helmets were all the boys wanted and they promised Santa that they had both been very good this year.

There is nothing in the whole year that comes close to being as exciting as Christmas Eve. You could take every school holiday, every birthday party and every cinema trip and roll them into one great day and they still wouldn't be half as good as Christmas Eve!

And the best part of the best night of the year is lying there in bed wide-awake but still dreaming of seeing your presents the next morning. And that's what Billy and Jimmy Brown were doing that night, until they fell asleep.

Dreaming of bicycles.

Waking first the next morning, Billy shook his brother hard and shouted, 'Get up lazy, it's Christmas!' Then, wild with excitement, they both ran in to call their parents. This was no time for a lie-in!

All four members of the Brown family rushed downstairs to see if Santa had brought everything he was supposed to.

Jimmy could see it as soon as the door opened! The most beautiful bike he had ever seen, sitting in his corner of the room. It was shiny and silver, just as it had been in his dreams and beside it on the sitting-room floor lay the coolest helmet ever made.

'Billy, look what I got!' he shouted as he turned to hug his brother. But Billy wasn't smiling.

Jimmy turned around and looked at Billy's corner, but all that he could see lying there was a helmet, a football and a note. There was no bicycle.

Billy picked up the note. 'It's from Santa,' he said and began to read:

My dear Billy,

I hope this finds you well.
Happy Christmas to you both.
As you can probably tell,
You are not getting everything
You asked me for this year.
For you have been a naughty boy
And word has reached my ear.
You let your brother take the blame
For something that you'd done.

It really was the two of you
He's not the only one!
So that is why you've got no bike
To cycle on today.
But I know your brother will share with you
Like you should have shared the blame!

But here's a promise I'll make to you
If you'll make one for me
Next Christmas Day you'll get your bike
If you're as good as you can be!

Santa

THE HEART-SHAPED BOX

SHIRLEY BENTON BAILEY

It wasn't easy being the oldest child at Christmas. Everyone was so interested in the twins' first Christmas that they'd completely forgotten about Hayley. And worst of all, even Santa had forgotten her!

It was four o'clock and Hayley had just crept downstairs to see what Santa had left her, only to find … nothing. Nothing for her, that was. Santa had left half of his toy factory for the twins. She knew, she just knew, that her parents hadn't even bothered posting her letter to Santa. If they remembered to feed her these days, she was doing well.

As she lay in bed, Hayley made a plan. She was going to run away later in the morning. She got up and packed a bag. As soon as it was bright, she was gone – where to, she

didn't know, but it would take her family so long to notice she'd even left that she'd have plenty of time to think of a good place.

She went back to bed and, as she drifted off to sleep, she heard a rustle. She looked up to see a face smiling at her.

'Santa! I thought you weren't coming this year!'

Santa's smile broadened. 'Why would you think that, my dear girl?'

Hayley explained how her parents were neglecting her, and how she was sure Santa wouldn't have received her letter.

Santa pulled two pieces of paper out of his pocket. He held one out to Hayley. 'This was the very first letter I received. Your parents must have sent it extra early.' Hayley looked at her own spidery handwriting.

'And this was the second,' Santa said as he handed Hayley the second letter.

'Dear Santa, please bring something extra special for Hayley this year. She's been such a big help to us with the new babies. Love, Hayley's parents.'

Santa reached into his sack and first pulled out a bag containing lots of circles in vibrant colours, then he produced something Hayley had once owned but had long since forgotten about.

'That's not a new present, Santa. That's the old box Daddy made for me last year!'

Hayley pouted as Santa handed the pink heart-shaped box to her. Her Dad, a carpenter, had made it for Hayley's jewellery, but she hadn't wanted it. It was plain, and she'd wanted one like her friend Sonya's, with a pop-up ballerina.

'Look around, Hayley. Do you really need a new present?' Santa gestured towards the dust-covered toy boxes stacked in a corner. 'Now, I've been watching you recently, and I'm afraid you think your parents love the twins more than they love you. Am I right?'

Hayley nodded.

'Well, Santa can tell you that your parents love you more than ever. But I don't expect you to just take my word for it, Hayley. That's why this old present will show you just how much you're loved.'

He pushed the box and the bag into her hands. 'I want you to think back on all the things your parents have done for you since the babies were born. For every one, put a circle into this box. It won't be long until you see for yourself that the babies' arrival hasn't changed a thing.'

He stood up. 'Happy Christmas, Hayley,' he whispered as he crept out of the room.

Hayley put the box under her pillow and settled down. As she slept, her mind filled with memories of things she'd done with her parents recently – the zoo, the fair, the circus. In her dream she could see herself opening the box and dropping circles into it. It wasn't long before it was full to

the brim, even though she had plenty more circles to put into it if she'd had room.

'Hayley, quick!' Hayley awoke to her mother's excited voice. 'Santa came!'

Hayley felt a rush of disappointment as her mother pulled her out of bed. Meeting Santa … getting the box … it had all just been a dream. She'd felt so cherished as she'd filled the box with symbols of her parents' love. Now, it was back to listening to the babies cry all day …

Hayley's mother led her out to the garage. 'Look!' she squealed, pointing at a shiny pink bike. Hayley gasped. It was amazing – a really grown-up bike, exactly what she wanted without even knowing she'd wanted it. Santa was a clever guy.

But happy as she was with her present, something was niggling at her. That dream had just felt so real …

She ran to her room and tossed her pillow aside. This time, she didn't gasp so much as wheeze in shock.

There it was, sitting proudly on her bed – the battered, wooden, heart-shaped box, overflowing with circles.

Hayley kicked her packed bag under her bed. Maybe home wasn't such a bad place after all …

CRYSTAL

MARIAN O'NEILL

Crystal remembered very little about being small. But she thought that that made sense. The bigger you were the more room you had for storing memories. She was big now. Her top branches scraped the winter sky, her roots tickled the rock of the forest floor and her skirt of pine needles jostled against the trees on either side of her.

And she was big enough to hold lots of memories. She remembered the steel grey cold of winter and the fluttering warmth of spring. She remembered the robin that had nestled in close to her tummy and the cloud of butterflies that once tickled the tips of her branches. She remembered growing away from the chattering, giggling bunches of bluebells, but most of all she remembered being lonely.

When she was little she had looked up to the trees that grew around her and had waited for the wind to rustle through her and carry her questions up to them.

'What is that so blue up so high?' she would ask.

'Who are they, flying by?' she would sigh.

'Are you my family?' she would cry.

But all around her those solid tree trunks stood tall and quiet. Now that Crystal was bigger she could see that they were very different from her. They wore their branches higher up than hers and they had no skirt of needles. In winter they dropped all their leaves and started again with a new coat in the spring. Crystal thought that they must be very cold, but they never complained, they never spoke at all, even when the wind whistled through them.

So she stopped talking to them and, instead, busied herself making friends with the creatures that came her way: the squirrels and birds and insects and foxes. Some came for a season, some just for a rest, but they all moved on again and every time they left, Crystal became a little lonelier.

So she tried to stop missing them and, instead, busied herself with games. At night she stretched as hard as she could to try and touch a star. Whenever the wind rustled through her she chattered all her needles together in an effort to sing and in the winter she spread all her needles out in the frost trying to coat every one of them with ice.

And that was how she got her name. It was the robin

nestling in her tummy that told her that she sparkled just like a crystal.

But still, Crystal was sad. Every winter seemed a little longer, every friendship a little shorter. Then, one cold, dark, blustery day Crystal heard the strangest sounds. A clump, clump, clumping. A rumble roar of laughter and a high shriek of delight.

'Oh this one Daddy please, can we have this one?'

Crystal looked down and saw three strange-looking animals, on their hind legs without much fur at all but with very pretty coverings. The big one made the rumbling laugh again and then he landed a thump against Crystal. She tottered and teetered, and felt another blow, and another and then, strangely enough, she was lying down. The creatures picked her up, very gently, and carried her to a big machine with wheels. They strapped her tight on top and whizzed her through the night.

It was the most exciting feeling Crystal had ever felt. There was so much wind that it fairly emptied her of words and songs. And then, suddenly, it was over. The machine shuddered and stopped, doors thudded, and the rumblings and shrieks were mingled with a calm, cooing voice.

'Oh come on in,' it said. 'It's so cold out here.'

Crystal couldn't believe it when the same gentle hands picked her up and carried her with them into their nest. They gave her a lovely drink of water and then tucked her

up into a cosy bed of fresh, warm earth, and then it was like all Crystal's dreams had come true.

They sang, slow, warm, happy songs just like the ones Crystal sang out on the wind, and they began to decorate her branches with all the memories she kept of her friends: paper butterflies, a fat snuggled robin, all kinds of bells – not just blue ones – and, on the tip of every branch, a strand of glittering frost.

And then, oh and then, the rumbly creature picked up the smallest of all the creatures and she stretched as high as she could and placed a star right on the tip of Crystal's top branch.

'Look,' the calm voice cooed, 'look, she's sparkling just like a crystal.'

And Crystal twinkled all her pines in gratitude and happiness. She had finally found her family and they had finally brought her home.

THE PASSING

EDDIE HOBBS

The old king's eyes were closed. He was near the end. His breathing had slowed and every time he paused before gulping in another long intake of air, the family at his bedside squeezed their hands together. The queen and his children, the four princes and princesses, had been joined by his twelve grandchildren as the vigil continued throughout its third night. The room was full of love but no great sadness. Everyone agreed that he'd lived a long and successful life – he'd ruled wisely.

He could hear them whisper in low tones close by, and he could feel their breaths as they each took turns to hold his hand, faces wet with tears, to say goodbye. The king's brow creased and frowned, which the family and doctors mistook for discomfort, but the old man wasn't in any

pain. Instead, he was puzzled. Throughout his long life he'd
tried to be virtuous, to live without causing harm, to love
his family and his people. But he knew there were many
times he'd made wrong choices, confusing the knowledge
so abundant among his many advisors, for true wisdom.
He knew he'd made poor decisions at times and there was
much to regret.

Now he faced the most important question of his life
– what happens now? Is this where it all ends? The religious
leaders had told him otherwise but could offer no proof, just
faith and like him, he thought, they too were human and
prone to errors. It was close now, he could feel it. He wasn't
afraid, just uncertain about what his life had really meant.

But just then he felt something ageless enter the room,
something as familiar to him as the wind, as deep as the
oceans and as endless as the stars. The king wasn't afraid,
just curious and strangely warm. He could feel a light like a
ball of pure energy growing next to him.

Then a voice, which seemed to have been fashioned out
of brightness itself, spoke in a tone as clear as mountain air:
'What are you?' the voice asked gently.

What a strange question, the king thought, before he
replied, 'I am King.'

'But what are you?' the voice asked again.

'I am flesh and blood, nothing more,' the king replied.

Then the voice said quite slowly, 'You are much more, you

confuse this failing body with your true nature. Now you return to the perfect centre of everything.'

Then the king asked, 'But who are you?'

The voice replied softly, 'I was once the wife of a carpenter.'

And at that the family at his side saw the king raise his right hand slowly as if he were going, and he drew his last breath. The king smiled his last words, 'You are the mother of The Preacher.'

CHRISTMAS WISHES

JACINTA MCDEVITT

It was nearly Christmas time; all the toys in the toyshop were very excited. They knew it was nearly Christmas time because Felicity Christmas Fairy had told them and Felicity Christmas Fairy knew everything there was to know about Christmas. She even knew Santa and Mrs Claus and had been to the North Pole for tea. So, you can see how she knew everything about Christmas.

Felicity knew it was nearly Christmas because the old toymaker who owned the beautiful toyshop she lived in had finished making all the toys for Christmas. The last bit of paint on the very last toy was just dry and the toymaker was able to put it on the last space left on the shelf. It was a blue train with 'Christmas Train' painted along the side of it. The toymaker knew some girl or boy would love it.

The toymaker was very excited and all the toys were very excited too because they knew that soon they would be going to little girls and boys who would play with them and love them.

The toymaker started singing, 'We wish you a merry Christmas, we wish you a merry Christmas', as he looked at all the toys arranged on the shelf. The toys looked fantastic. The toymaker was delighted with all his work.

'Time to put up the Christmas decorations,' he said as he dragged a big box out of the attic.

The toys looked on as the toymaker hung tinsel from all the shelves. He hung bright red baubles with long golden ribbons in the shop window and put a big sign outside the shop: 'HAPPY CHRISTMAS. TOYS FOR SALE'.

Then the toymaker put up a beautiful Christmas tree and hung bright lights all around it. Red, green, purple, blue and yellow, they winked and flashed on the tree. He reached up high to the very top shelf in the toyshop and took Felicity Christmas Fairy down. Her long white dress was trimmed with fur and her silver wings sparkled in the light. The toymaker placed Felicity carefully on the top of the Christmas tree.

All the toys looked at her. She was so beautiful.

'You look beautiful up there on the top of the tree,' said Teddy Bear.

'Amazing.'

'Gorgeous.'

'So Christmassy,' said all the toys.

'Thank you all. This is my most favourite job you know. I love being the fairy on top of the Christmas tree.'

Just then the door to the toyshop opened and a man came in.

'Hi,' he said to the toymaker.

'Hello. How can I help you?' asked the toymaker.

'I am looking for two dolls to give my two daughters for Christmas.'

The dolls on the doll shelf all started giggling with excitement. They knew two of them were going to be chosen for the two little girls for Christmas.

The toymaker took the dolls down off their shelf. He laid them out along the counter and held them up one by one.

'This one is Amelia; she has long blond hair and blue eyes. This next one is Colleen and she has red hair and green eyes. These next two are sisters. One is called Rosie and the other is Stephanie. Both of them have black curly hair and big brown eyes.' The toymaker described each one.

'They are all lovely. But these two are perfect! Two beautiful sister dolls for two beautiful sisters. I will take Rosie and Stephanie. My girls will love them. Can you wrap them up for me please?'

'Yes. Of course.'

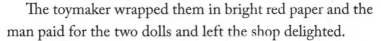

The toymaker wrapped them in bright red paper and the man paid for the two dolls and left the shop delighted.

Next into the shop came a lady and a man and they wanted four toys for their four children.

'I hope they pick me,' the little train said.

'Oh! They might pick me,' a beautiful little toy robin perched high up on a shelf said. The robin was hoping that someone would buy him. He wanted to hear all the Christmas songs and be put on the mantelpiece to see all the best things about Christmas: the crib with the little baby Jesus, the turkey, the pudding, Christmas cake and Christmas crackers and all the other Christmas things. The robin loved Christmas.

'You should make a Christmas wish, Robin,' Teddy Bear suggested.

'That's a great idea. I will. I will make a Christmas wish now.' Robin closed his eyes tightly. 'I wish, I wish that some-one would buy me and bring me home for Christmas.'

'That should work,' Teddy Bear said, smiling at Robin.

'Don't worry Robin,' Felicity Christmas Fairy said. 'Someone will come in and be looking for you. Wait and see.'

But the man and woman pointed to the toys they wanted to buy for their children and the robin wasn't one of them.

'Can we have that train, the blue ball, that lovely pink tea set and the tractor?'

'Hooray! I'm off,' said the tractor.

'Me too,' said the ball as he bounced around the toy-shop.

'Who'd like a nice cup of tea before we go?' asked the tea set.

'No time for that. We're going. Bye everyone, Happy Christmas,' said the train.

The toymaker wrapped them all up in Christmas paper and wished the lady and man a very Happy Christmas.

'And a very Happy Christmas to you and all your family.'

The shop was quiet again. But not for long. People came in and out all day long. All sorts of people looking for all sorts of toys for their family and friends.

The little robin still sat on the shelf, waiting. He was afraid his wish wasn't working so he wished it again. He closed his eyes tightly.

'I wish, I wish I could be all wrapped up for someone for Christmas.'

But the day went on into the evening and the little robin still sat on the shelf as one by one all the other toys were sold and went. Even Teddy Bear, Robin's best friend was gone. A tiny little tear fell from Robin's eyes. He fluffed up his feathers and stuck out his bright red chest. Then he felt a strong, loving hand around him. The toymaker lifted the robin down off the shelf.

'Come down here,' he said. 'No one can see you up there. A beautiful robin should be seen by everyone at Christmas.'

He took the robin and put him in the centre of the window in among all the beautiful Christmas balls and golden ribbons.

Robin looked out the window and saw it was dark outside. All the trees in the village were covered in sparkling coloured lights. Snow was on the ground and light snowflakes were falling all around. People were rushing home to hang up their stockings in time for Santa Claus.

Just then two beautiful little girls came running up to the window. They pressed their faces right up against the glass and stared in at Robin.

Robin looked out at them. He had never seen such beautiful big blue eyes before. He was delighted when the girls smiled in at him.

The snow started to fall harder and Robin could see the girls were well muffled up. They were wearing red Wellington boots and red coats. The coats looked really cosy and warm. They had white gloves and hats on and each little girl was wearing a white scarf. They kept pointing in at him.

Then one of the little girls said: 'Look, Chloe! Isn't it just what we wished for?'

'Yes, yes, Alannah. It is exactly what we wished for.'

'It's perfect,' the two girls said together.

'Let's go in.'

'Well, hello young ladies. Who have we here?'

'I'm Alannah.'

'I'm Chloe.'

'It's a pleasure to meet such beautiful girls,' the toymaker said. 'Now tell me Alannah and Chloe will you be hanging up your stockings for Santa Claus tonight?'

'Definitely. We are definitely hanging up our stockings for Santa Claus,' the two little girls nodded.

'I'm delighted to hear that,' said the toymaker. 'Now tell me what can I do for you?'

'We were looking all over the village for a very special Christmas present for our Gran and Granddad,' said Alannah.

'We looked everywhere but we couldn't find anything special enough,' said Chloe.

'Oh dear,' said the toymaker.

'We closed our eyes tightly and wished and wished to find something special and now we have found it.'

Alannah was nearly bursting with excitement and she jumped up and down pointing at the window.

'Definitely. We have found it. Our wishes came true.'

Chloe was just as excited and she too was jumping up and down and pointing at the window.

'It's the robin in your window.' The two girls pointed again, 'Can we have it please?'

'Of course you can. He's a real beauty isn't he?'

Robin couldn't believe it. He was delighted when he was lifted from the window and wrapped up in gold paper with gold ribbons as Alannah and Chloe counted out all their pocket money and gave it to the toymaker.

'I'm sure your Gran and Granddad will like their robin.'

'They won't just like it, they'll love it. They will put it in a special place on the mantelpiece for Christmas,' Alannah and Chloe said.

'A very Happy Christmas to you,' said the toymaker.

'A very Happy Christmas to you,' said Alannah.

'A very Happy Christmas to you,' said Chloe.

'A very Happy Christmas for me too,' said Robin.

'And a very Happy Christmas to all of you,' said Felicity Christmas Fairy as she waved her magic wand.

JIMMY'S DAD

ROISIN MEANEY

Jimmy was seven years old and he lived at the North Pole with his Mum and Dad. Jimmy's Mum was a small, jolly lady who loved to bake. Every day she baked apple tarts and pineapple upside-down cakes and chocolate muffins and raspberry buns. Jimmy's Dad was a big, round man with a fluffy white beard who loved to eat. Every day he ate all the delicious things that Jimmy's Mum made and every day he grew a little rounder.

Jimmy's Dad had a very important job. He was the boss of a giant toy factory where all kinds of toys were made all year long. Hundreds of workers made thousands of toys – trucks and dolls and robots and cars and yo-yos and drums and fire engines and jigsaws and clockwork mice – and just about every other toy you could think of. Jimmy's Dad was a very kind boss and all the workers in the toy factory loved him almost as much as Jimmy did.

Every Christmas Eve Jimmy's Mum baked an extra special fruitcake, full of raisins and honey and nuts and cherries. While she was baking her special cake, Jimmy's Dad put on his very best red suit and his big black belt and his big black boots and his red hat with the white fur all around it. Then he got the biggest sack in the world and he filled it right to the top with all the toys his workers had made all year long.

When the sack was full he loaded it onto his sleigh and he called his twelve reindeer and harnessed them to the sleigh. Then he ate a big slice of the extra special fruitcake that Jimmy's Mum had baked. After that he sat into his sleigh and waved goodbye to Jimmy and his Mum, and gave the signal for his reindeer to go.

And every Christmas Eve the reindeer galloped across the snow, faster and faster until all at once their hooves left the ground and they were flying! Jimmy and his Mum watched as the sleigh climbed higher and higher into the starry sky. They watched until it was just a tiny little dot far, far away, and then they went back inside and switched on the telly and made hot chocolate.

Have you guessed who Jimmy's Dad is?

That's right, he is Santa!

Jimmy's Dad was the most famous Dad in the whole

world, and Jimmy was very proud of him. He was so happy that his Dad went all around the world every Christmas Eve, bringing toys to every single boy and girl. And of course every year Jimmy got a toy too; his very favourite toy from the whole factory!

One Christmas Eve, just before Jimmy's eighth birthday, Jimmy's Dad set off in his sleigh as usual. Jimmy and his Mum waved goodbye like they always did and then went back inside and made hot chocolate. Just as Jimmy was finishing off his hot chocolate, his mobile phone rang. It was his Dad calling.

'Hi Dad,' he said. 'Everything OK?'

'I'm afraid not,' his Dad answered. 'I've just started delivering my toys, but I'm stuck in a chimney and I need help. I'm sending Rudolph back to get you, so put on your warmest clothes and wait for him.'

Jimmy was so excited! Ever since he was a very small boy he'd wanted to go in the sleigh with his Dad, but he'd never been allowed. Now at last it was going to happen! He ran upstairs and dressed in his woolliest, furriest clothes, and then he went downstairs to wait for his Dad's best reindeer to come and collect him. A few minutes later he heard the sound of galloping hooves and he opened the door to find Rudolph standing there.

'Hurry – climb on my back!' Rudolph called. 'There's no time to lose!'

Jimmy climbed onto the reindeer's back, his heart beating fast.

'Be careful dear,' his Mum called as Rudolph began to gallop across the snow, faster and faster until at last they took off! Jimmy held on tightly as Rudolph climbed higher and higher into the starry sky. He watched his Mum until she was just a tiny dot in the middle of the snow. His heart was beating as loudly as a drum as he flew through the air, passing twinkly stars, round planets and small puffy clouds.

In no time at all they reached the first house. Rudolph landed on the roof beside all the other reindeer. Jimmy climbed off his back and ran to the chimney.

'Dad?' he called.

'Grab my hand and pull me up!' his Dad answered. Jimmy reached down and grabbed his Dad's hand and pulled and pulled with all his might – and his Dad popped out of the chimney like a cork from a bottle!

'Phew – thanks son,' he said, brushing the soot from his best red suit. 'I thought I was going to be stuck down there until next Christmas!'

'How will you get the presents down?' Jimmy asked.

'I won't – you will!' his Dad replied. 'You'll have to be my messenger and deliver the presents to every house, and I'll wait on the roof with the reindeer.'

Jimmy couldn't believe it – he was going to be doing the

most important job in the whole world! Quick as a flash he grabbed the presents from his Dad and slid down the chimney, and before you could say, 'Humpty Dumpty had a great fall', he was back up on the roof.

'That was very quick indeed,' his Dad smiled. Jimmy felt so proud he thought he'd burst. All night long they worked, delivering millions of presents to every single boy and girl. When they had finished, Jimmy was very, very tired. His Dad smiled at him.

'You are the best helper I could ever have,' he said. 'Here, climb into the sleigh and we'll be home in no time.'

Jimmy climbed in and closed his eyes, and before the reindeer had even taken off he was fast asleep!

When they got home Jimmy's Mum was waiting for them. She took one look at Jimmy's Dad and said, 'I think we'll have to put you on a diet.'

Jimmy's Dad patted his round tummy and smiled. 'I think you're right,' he said. 'No more pineapple upside-down cakes for me!'

And from then on, Jimmy's Mum only baked on Sundays and Jimmy's Dad just had a small slice, and by the time Christmas came around again, he was just the right size for all the chimneys.

But every night when Jimmy goes to sleep he remembers the very best night of his life, when he had the most important job in the whole world.

GETTING BETTER

GERALDINE O'NEILL

Even though it was the week before the Christmas holidays, it was a bright sunny day and the frost was melting.

Danny was happy because that meant the children would be allowed to play football at break time.

Danny's Mammy stopped the car outside the school gate. 'Have a great day,' she told him. 'And Daddy and I can't wait to see you playing Santa Claus next week in the Christmas play.' She smiled. 'And Granny and Granddad are so proud they're going to come up from Tullamore for it.'

'That'll be great!' Danny said. He loved his grandparents. He saw them every other weekend. They must think his part in the Christmas play was really special to travel up to Dublin in the middle of the week.

Mammy gave him a quick kiss. She always did it in the

car because the boys teased each other if they saw things like that. As he opened the door, his mother said. 'Be good. Do your work and don't get into any trouble.'

Danny smiled back at her and then ran off to join his friends in the yard.

When they got into the classroom all the children were delighted when they saw that Miss Rabbitte had hung the Christmas lanterns they had made on a long string across the class. She had also stuck the cheery painted snowmen with the black hats and orange noses onto the windows.

The teacher switched on the sparkling lights on their Christmas tree and then gave the children a few minutes to look at all the nice things in the class. Then she clapped her hands and they all sat down to do their work.

English and Irish in the morning went OK. Danny had learned his spellings and got them all right. He was also able to do the two pages in his Irish workbook.

The problems started when Miss Rabbitte told them to take out their maths workbooks. Danny found maths very hard and he always worried about it. His Dad had helped him with his homework the night before, which was adding sums with a carrying figure.

Danny was happy because he was sure that he would remember how to do them now. He took his book out and then Miss Rabbitte told them to swap with the person next to them. He gave his book to Ellie and she gave him hers.

The teacher called out the answers to the homework sums and, as he ticked all Ellie's, he kept trying to see if his were OK. His Dad had said they were fine, but he still couldn't help worrying.

Miss Rabbitte called out the last sum and Ellie handed his book back. He looked at the pages and a big smile grew on his face. He had gotten 10 out of 10! He was really happy and felt he must be getting better at maths.

Miss Rabbitte went to the board now and started talking about fractions. 'If you remember,' she told the children, 'we did these a few weeks ago, and I want to see if you remember them.'

She gave them all a worksheet with twenty fractions. 'If you get stuck, come up to my desk and I'll help you.'

Ten minutes later, Danny was still looking at an empty worksheet with squares, circles, triangles and rectangles. He was supposed to colour in a half or a quarter of each and write the name under them.

But Danny couldn't remember what a half and a quarter was.

'Is the half the bigger one?' he whispered to Ellie.

'I'm not telling you,' she said and stuck her tongue out at him. 'Go up and ask the teacher.'

But Danny didn't want to walk up to the front of the class. Everyone would know he needed help and would think he was stupid.

Danny tried to pull Ellie's workbook across the table to look at, but Ellie just pulled it back.

'They're easy,' Ellie whispered. 'A one-year-old baby could do them!'

Danny suddenly felt very stupid. He reached up and pulled Ellie's blond ponytail.

'Yow!' Ellie said and pinched Danny back on the knee.

Miss Rabbitte looked up from the class register. 'Keep the noise down,' she said, and went back to her work.

Very soon Miss Rabbitte started going around the groups, ticking everyone's work. Danny knew that she would soon be at his desk and she would see that he hadn't even started his work. He began to feel all hot and worried.

He looked at the squares and the circles again and then he started to colour what he thought was a half of one of the squares. When Miss Rabbitte wasn't looking he squinted over at Ellie's and saw she had coloured in more of the square than he had.

Ellie's work would be right.

Ellie got most things right! Sometimes he felt like hitting her.

Danny could hear Miss Rabbitte's voice behind him and his heart began to beat quicker. He looked up at the clock on the wall and saw that the hands were almost on 11 o'clock. He was getting better at telling the time, and he knew that the bell would go for playtime in about a minute.

Then, Miss Rabbitte came to Ellie's desk. She looked at the worksheet. 'Good girl,' she said. She started to tick the coloured-in shapes with her red pen.

Danny knew he was next. Quick as a flash – he swiped Ellie's *High School Musical* pencil case off the desk and onto the floor.

'You did that on purpose!' Ellie's face was very angry. 'You better pick it up!'

'I didn't ...' Danny said. His face started to go red because he knew he was telling a lie.

'Danny!' Miss Rabbitte's voice was cross. 'Don't deny it. I saw you throw that pencil case with my own eyes.'

Danny put his head down and said nothing. He hated getting in trouble, but he would have felt much worse if she had seen his empty worksheet.

He couldn't tell Miss Rabbitte that he couldn't do fractions because she would think he was stupid. Then everyone else in the class would hear and they would think he was stupid too. He would rather get into trouble for messing around than have everyone think he was a dunce at maths.

The bell rang.

'OK everyone,' Miss Rabbitte said, clapping her hands. 'If you didn't get your worksheet finished, do it for homework and I'll check it tomorrow.' She looked at Danny and sighed. 'You wait behind. You'll have to miss your break now for your bad behaviour.'

Miss Rabbitte told the girls they could leave the class first for break time since they had lined up without any pushing or shoving. Then the boys were allowed to go. Danny was standing in the corner. He turned to look as the boys disappeared through the door, and saw Ruairí Hynes carrying the football under his arm.

Danny gave a big sigh. He loved football. That was one of the things he was good at. That and acting in the Christmas play.

He looked across to the computer corner where Brainbox Colin was doing a maths programme with his headphones on. The ordinary class lessons were far too easy for him. Colin hated noise and liked to work on his own, writing stories or doing complicated projects.

He was allowed to stay in during the breaks because all the other kids running around laughing and shouting made him bad tempered. An older teacher, Mrs White, came in every day to sit with him and sometimes they played difficult games like chess.

Miss Rabbitte lifted her handbag. 'Danny,' she said in a disappointed voice, 'this is the second playtime you've had to miss this week because you've been messing about. When are you going to learn to behave?'

Danny looked down at his shoes. He liked Miss Rabbitte and he always felt guilty when her voice sounded sad.

'I'm sorry,' Danny said.

'Ellie told me that you tried to pull her book off her and when she wouldn't let you, you pulled her ponytail.' She raised her eyebrows. 'And I saw you throw her pencil case across the floor with my own eyes.'

Danny moved from one foot to the other. How could he tell his teacher that he had been trying to copy from Ellie because he didn't understand what he was supposed to do?

Miss Rabbitte lifted her handbag and said, 'I don't like keeping you in, Danny, because I know you love playing football but you need to learn to behave.' She shook her head. 'If you keep on being silly, I'm afraid I'm going to have to take you out of the school play. We can't have a silly Santa on the stage. How would your Mammy and Daddy feel if they saw you messing around and throwing things?'

Danny's face fell. He hadn't thought that getting in trouble might make him lose his part in the play. His Mammy and Daddy would be very upset. And he'd feel terrible if they had to tell Granny and Granddad not to come.

A new teacher that Danny didn't know came to the door. He was quite small and he was wearing a tracksuit. He looked like somebody who was good at sports.

'I'm Mr Ryan. Miss White is sick,' he said, 'so I'm here to keep Colin company.'

'We have two boys in for break today,' Miss Rabbitte said. She whispered to the new teacher for a few minutes, and Danny knew she was talking about him and Colin.

Miss Rabbitte lifted up some worksheets from the table and showed them to the teacher. They both walked down to the corner where Colin was and Miss Rabbitte tapped him on the shoulder. Colin took off his headphones and listened while she explained about Miss White being sick and about Mr Ryan being there today. Then Miss Rabbitte left to get her coffee and biscuits with the other teachers.

'Hi lads,' Mr Ryan said, giving them a friendly thumbs-up. 'Your teacher said we might look at some fractions on the computer.'

Danny's heart sank. Great! He was going to have to work during his break now.

Mr Ryan looked at Colin. 'Can you find us a programme that starts at the very beginning?'

Colin stared at the computer. Sometimes he didn't like looking at people. 'Do you mean basic shapes and things?'

'That would be great,' Mr Ryan said.

Colin started looking through a pile of computer games. Danny looked out of the window, through the space between the stuck-on snowmen, and he could see the lads playing football. He watched as Ruairí Hynes scored a goal and all the lads ran around cheering.

He wished he was playing with them.

Mr Ryan turned to Danny. 'Miss Rabbitte said she wasn't sure if you had finished your worksheet and she asked me to help you.'

Danny wondered if Miss Rabbitte had guessed he was stuck at his work. He suddenly felt awkward. 'I don't like fractions,' he said.

'I think you'll find it more fun if we look at how it works on the computer first.'

Danny looked at him. He couldn't imagine anything about fractions being fun.

'Is this OK?' Colin asked, without looking at them.

They all looked at the computer screen and there was a brightly coloured game on it with all different shapes dancing around with faces on them. A funny voice started to explain that a half of anything meant one part out of two. It then showed you half an apple, half a bar of chocolate and half a cake. Then the funny voice told you to point the mouse at a colour and it would colour in a half of all the shapes.

Colin explained to Danny how to colour in the shapes and then he stood up. 'They're too easy for me. I'll let you have the computer chair.'

Danny's face went red because Colin had said the sums were easy. He wanted to say something smart back to Brainbox Colin, but he didn't want to get into trouble with Mr Ryan. He sat down in the chair and then moved the mouse to colour all the halves in.

'That's good,' Colin said. 'You know halves now. I'll move it onto quarters for you now.' He leaned over and clicked

on the mouse. 'You'll be grand if you remember that it only means 1 out of 4. A third means 1 out of 3, and so on.'

The first time Danny coloured in the quarter correctly, the computer made a cheering noise and Colin started clapping along with it.

'Well done!' Mr Ryan said.

Five minutes later, there was a big smile on Danny's face. He knew how to colour in halves, quarters, thirds and sixths. He would be able to do his fractions worksheet tonight without any trouble. The way Colin had explained it to him made it seem easy. He had picked the right computer game for him.

The bell went for the children to come back inside.

'Thanks, Mr Ryan,' Danny said.

Mr Ryan nodded over to Colin.

'Thanks, Colin,' Danny said. 'You're brilliant at computers. You're brilliant at all your work.'

'I'm good at some things,' Colin said. 'But I'm not good at sports. You're the best footballer in the class. People can be good at different things. Isn't that right, Mr Ryan?'

'Indeed it is,' the teacher said.

Danny thought for a moment. It was true. Colin wasn't good at football. He wasn't very good at throwing and catching balls either. All the noise and the shouting outside made it hard for him to concentrate. Danny wondered if not being able to catch a ball made Colin get upset, the way

he got upset about his maths. He'd never thought about it before.

All the other children came back in now and got their lunches out.

Miss Rabbitte came down to the computer corner and Mr Ryan explained how good Danny and Colin had been, and how much they'd enjoyed the fraction game.

'I got them all right, Miss,' Danny said. 'I understand the halves and quarters now and even the thirds. Colin and Mr Ryan helped me.'

'I'm delighted,' Miss Rabbitte said, smiling at him.

Miss Rabbitte told him and Colin to go and get their lunch and then the two teachers stood chatting while the children were eating. When lunch was over, Miss Rabbitte called Colin and Danny outside the classroom door. Danny's heart sank. He wondered if he was in more trouble.

'Mr Ryan has quarter of an hour to spare now,' Miss Rabbitte said, 'and he's just suggested that you two boys might like to go into the hall with him.'

Mr Ryan looked at the boys. 'I thought that since Colin helped Danny with his maths, that Danny might like to help Colin with his throwing and catching skills. What do you think?'

Colin shrugged and said, 'OK.'

A big grin came over Danny's face. 'Brilliant!' he said. He suddenly felt that he liked Colin now. And it would be ace

to get out of class for a while to play around. To play around, not mess around.

They had a great game in the hall and when Colin caught the basketball three times in a row, Danny gave him a big cheer.

As they were walking back to the classroom, Mr Ryan put a hand on both boys' shoulders. 'Colin is getting better at sports,' he said, 'and Danny is getting better at maths. You can't be brilliant at everything – but if you keep practising at things you'll definitely get better.'

Colin smiled. 'My brothers ask me to play ball with them but I never want to because I'm no good at it. I'm going to try harder.'

'And I'm going to try harder at my maths,' Danny said, smiling.

From now on he would do things properly. If he didn't know something in class he would ask Miss Rabbitte instead of messing about. Thanks to Colin, he now realised that people can't be perfect at everything. But if you practise, you can get better.

He wouldn't get into any more trouble now. He would make sure he did his very best for the Christmas play.

He would practise his lines until they were perfect so Mammy and Daddy, and Granny and Granddad would be proud of him.

He would be the best Santa Claus ever.

The Christmas Tree

PATRICIA SCANLAN

I couldn't make up my mind whether to put up a Christmas tree or not this year. It seemed like a lot of trouble when I was going to be here on my own. Don't get me wrong, I had invites to spend Christmas with family, but did you ever just want to stay at home in your own house and sleep in your own bed?

I can understand of course why my son and daughter don't like the idea too much. When I was their age if my own widowed eighty-year-old mother had refused my invitation to spend Christmas with my family and me, I would have been upset and worried at her being alone on Christmas Day.

I've spent the last decade trotting between their houses for Christmas. And while I love them, and my five grandchildren – and have spent many Christmases with them since my much-loved husband, Lorcan, passed away – this year I have a yearning to stay at home.

I haven't bought a turkey. I don't really care for it. The only part I like is the dark meat under the legs. Instead I've bought a fillet steak. I'll fry onions and potatoes with it. That will be a tasty dinner with little fuss. I've cooked a ham though, so I'll have meat to make a sandwich for visitors.

As I say, I'd dithered about putting up a tree. It seemed like a lot of hassle. But then when I saw the gleaming lights in windows in the village I was sorry I'd told my daughter not to bother.

It came up in conversation with my new neighbour, Sarah. She and her husband, Will, bought the dormer bungalow next door. I couldn't ask for nicer neighbours. I met Sarah at the post office and complimented her on the lovely lights she has on the chestnut tree in the front garden. That was how we got into a conversation about the Christmas tree. Well, an hour later, there was a knock on the door and it was Will. Now between you and me, if I was forty years younger, he's exactly the type of man I'd have fallen for. He's the tall, lean, rangy type. Like my own dear Lorcan. A manly sort of man, not like these young chaps today who have too much to say for themselves, and who spend half their lives sitting at computers with their nets and their twitters and emails and the like.

Will is an electrician. He has his own company and is doing well, even in the recession. His father is a farmer and Will helps out on the farm. He has the look of it, a real outdoors type with a strong face and the bluest of blue eyes.

'Mrs Kenny,' he said, standing at my door with his thumbs hooked into his jeans, 'Sarah tells me you can't decide about your Christmas tree. If I can be of any use at all, I'd be delighted to help out.'

'That's very kind of you,' I said, 'but I've left it too late to buy one, there'll only be rubbish left. I've always put up a real tree. My late husband had no truck with artificial ones. When I saw the one you have lit up in your garden I got a little nostalgic for one that's all. But thank you very much for offering.'

'No trouble at all.' He smiled. He has lovely glinting blue eyes, just like Lorcan. He waved from the gate and I waved back, warmed by his and Sarah's kindness.

Just before tea, there was a knock at my door. There was Will with the most beautiful, perfectly shaped Christmas tree. The scent of it brought back such memories. 'I have some lights too in case all yours aren't working,' he told me.

I was overwhelmed as he set to positioning it in the bay window, turning it this way and that for the best angle to show off its glory. Sarah came to help and between us we decorated it from the big box of baubles I had under the stairs.

They devoured the slices of baked ham I served them, on thick Vienna rolls slathered in butter, which we ate under the sparkling glow of the tree, with the fire crackling in the grate as the wind howled outside.

The tree is magnificent, the soft reds, blues, silver and greens of the lanterns reflecting on the baubles as they glisten and shimmer. I'm so delighted to have a tree and very touched by my neighbours' kindness. I sit up until late, admiring it.

'Nana you have a real tree.' My grandchildren are ecstatic when they call on Christmas Eve.

'Mum, I would have put it up for you,' Charlotte, my daughter chides.

'I wanted to surprise you,' I fib.

'It's beautiful, just like the ones Dad used to put up.'

We squeeze hands as sadness shadows us momentarily.

'I was thinking, I could cook dinner here if you'd like,' she offers. 'Then we'd all be together. And we could enjoy the tree.'

'Perfect!' I say, delighted with the suggestion. Christmas at home, what could be nicer?

'She must have had an inkling,' I hear Charlotte say to Sarah and Will. 'She was so insistent on staying at home this year.'

I gaze down at them as they follow the coffin into the church. My beloved Lorcan is by my side. I have never been happier. I am young and carefree again. It is dusk and the New Year is one day old. The Christmas tree lights sparkle in windows along the village, incandescent in the deepening night. My tree glows brightest of all.

Away From Home

JASON EDWARDS

Despite the fact that it was Christmas Eve, Stanley was not happy. He was not where he wanted to be, which was at his own home. Instead, his parents had brought him halfway across the country to stay with his grandparents for the holidays.

It was not that he disliked his grandparents, or disliked visiting them, but after a few hours he began to miss his own house. Here, he did not have his computer or a television with hundreds of channels to choose from or any of his toys, and there were no other children living nearby for him to play with their computer, or watch their television, or play with their toys.

'I miss my computer,' said Stanley, when his grandfather asked him what was wrong.

'A computer? Who needs a computer with all that snow outside?' His grandfather pointed at the back garden, which was covered in a soft blanket of white, fluffy snow. 'Come on, put your coat and gloves on and come with me.'

Stanley trudged outside behind his grandfather and stood with his arms folded across his chest.

'Now what?' Stanley asked.

'Close your eyes,' said his grandfather.

'Fine,' said Stanley, and shut his eyes. A second later he opened them again in surprise as a freezing cold ball of snow bounced off his nose. His grandfather was grinning from ear to ear and was already rolling up a second snowball in his hands. Stanley managed to dodge the second attack and scooped up his own handful of snow to throw at his grandfather.

When it had become too cold to stay outside, Stanley and his grandfather came back inside to warm themselves by the open fireplace. Stanley's grandmother handed them each a cup of hot chocolate with tiny marshmallows bobbing on the top and wrapped a blanket around both of them to keep them snug.

'I wish there was something good to watch on television,' said Stanley, looking at the television that had only a handful of channels to choose from unlike his own back home.

'You don't need television to be entertained,' said his grandmother. She walked across to a shelf and took a book

175

down. She sat down next to Stanley so that he was sandwiched warmly between his grandparents. His grandmother began to read from the book as Stanley sipped on his hot chocolate. He was so enthralled in the story that he did not notice the time flying by or that his parents had also joined them in the living room to listen. When his grandmother finished the tale, they gave her a round of applause for reading it so well and for using lots of different voices for the characters.

'Do you have any toys I could play with?' asked Stanley hopefully.

'I think we have some puzzles,' said his grandfather. He stood up and walked over to one of the shelves on the wall.

'A puzzle isn't a toy Granddad,' said Stanley, rolling his eyes.

'It is if you make a game of it,' said his grandfather. He took down a box and placed it on the coffee table. 'There, 2,000 pieces, I wonder how quickly we can get it done.'

'We'll get it done in no time if we work together,' said Stanley's father as he sat down next to the table where the adults began sifting through the puzzle pieces. Stanley watched them separating out the pieces for a few minutes before he decided that helping them was better than just sitting there and being bored doing nothing.

'Good job Stanley, you've found a corner piece,' exclaimed his mother, ruffling his hair with her hand.

'I remember the first time you helped me do a puzzle,'

said Stanley's grandfather to Stanley's father. 'You were about four and somehow managed to get a piece stuck up your nose.'

'Dad, you're so silly,' laughed Stanley.

'What? I just wanted to know if it would fit, and it did.' His father grinned.

'Yes, well I'm not sure the four hours we spent waiting in hospital for someone to remove it was worth all the hassle,' said Stanley's grandmother.

'It wasn't a piece from this puzzle was it?' asked Stanley, looking at the piece in his hand suspiciously.

'Oh no, we didn't keep that puzzle. The piece never fitted properly after that anyway,' said his grandfather.

'What other stupid things has he done?' asked Stanley eagerly.

'Well ...' said his grandmother, and then she and his grandfather began telling story after story of all the silly things that his father had ever done growing up, with each story being sillier and funnier than the previous one and sending everyone into fits of giggles.

Stanley smiled and looked around the room at the happy grinning faces. He didn't need his computer, or television channels, or toys, or his own house. His home was where his family were and that was all he needed to be happy.

An Interview with the Main Man in the Red Jersey

KEITH ANDREWS

As an Irish footballer living and working in the UK, I'm always chuffed to get letters and emails from family, friends and the odd fan or two or three … My most surprising letter arrived six weeks ago from a certain Mr S. Claus, sealed in a snow white envelope, complete with a North Pole stamp mark. Initially, I suspected another trick from my old pal Darren Costello, but this was no fake.

Mr Claus seemed to know me inside out and while I can't go into too much detail about the contents of my letter, Santa said he was glad I'd never stayed on the Naughty List for too long – especially after that little incident in 1988 and that he wasn't one bit surprised by my career choice, given my rolling request for a shiny new football for ten years in a row!

Indeed, I was pleasantly surprised to hear that Mr and Mrs Claus are soccer fans and they like nothing more on St Stephen's Day than to sit down and watch the football with their feet up. He had a few good tips for me to improve my game next season and suggested that I might consider working as a sports reporter in years to come as I was getting better at handling those post game interviews. Cheek! But that gave me an idea. What about an exclusive interview with the man in the Red Jersey for the Jack & Jill Christmas book? This is it.

KA: Where do you find the time to write letters to footballers and do interviews?

SC: Over the years our database system, which now contains over two billion addresses, has gotten faster and better. Now instead of writing our list out long hand, which took weeks and weeks, it's all computerised and, before you ask Keith, we do have a good backup system just in case the computer crashes. So that leaves more time for me and Mrs Claus to keep in touch with old friends. I don't do many interviews, certainly not on the record, but I decided to make an exception for you and for the Jack & Jill book.

KA: Some people say it's impossible to deliver billions of

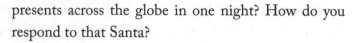

presents across the globe in one night? How do you respond to that Santa?

SC: I say nothing is impossible Keith, and you should know that. These people you're referring to – who are they? Have they forgotten about the magic of Christmas and without sounding ageist I bet it's the adults you're re-ferring to, right? Explaining everything in simple, neat terms is just not possible in my profession. What I can say is that my sleigh has a highly sophisticated, built-in navigation pulse that works in multi-dimensional time gears and my reindeers are showered in magic dust on departure and topped up regularly throughout the trip. I have an auto pilot should I need it and my elf transport department has an accurate tracker device at HQ. It's fast and it works, but the ins and outs are well beyond the scope of this interview. I would ask these people to close their eyes and open their minds. Sorry if that sounds a bit rude Keith!

KA: No problem Santa. An easy one now – what is your favourite colour?

SC: Red. I used to wear green a lot in the early days, but Mrs Claus says that red is my colour now.

KA: What is your favourite toy?

SC: Good question. I get to test play all the toys leaving

our secret workshops and I've seen lots of whizz bam toys over the years that don't last. My Top 4 are all classics – blocks, ball, book and board game. All Bs for some reason but A-plus toys in terms of family fun, performance and skill development. Oh, and jigsaws; I love a good jigsaw, as does Mrs Claus.

KA: How do you keep fit and still eat all the goodies left out on Christmas Eve?

SC: As part of my preparation I've got to build up an extra layer of insulation to keep me warm for my gruelling round trip and that means eating more calories than I burn throughout November and December in particular. However, Mrs Claus who keeps a close eye on everything – including my weight – has suggested that my BMI (Body Mass Index) is too high even for me! In fact, she's designing a Fit Fast programme for me in January – so I might be back to you for a few tips Keith. Contrary to what some people think, I do enjoy playing sport as well as watching it on TV and you wouldn't even recognise me if you bumped into me in mid summer. Of course, I can't eat every mince pie and cookie left by the children and I have to admit that some of the grown-ups actually eat some of the cookies before I arrive – which suits me fine. In most cases I wrap up and take away the best goodies and the elves and reindeer tuck in when we get home.

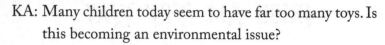

KA: Many children today seem to have far too many toys. Is this becoming an environmental issue?

SC: Yes. I am concerned about the trend of children getting so many toys throughout the year, so much so that they simply don't know what to ask for when it comes to Christmas time and some of them chop and change their letters three times and post their letters way too late, which creates logistical problems for us. A simple Toy Audit every September would help a lot and I would encourage everyone to reduce, reuse and recycle for sustainable toy management. I welcome the trend in many households to reduce the number of toys being asked for – that certainly works for me and it's better for the environment. However, I would say that the children today are very environmentally aware, much more so than their parents, and they'll work it out.

KA: Finally, Santa if you weren't doing your current job, what would you do?

SC: Now that's a tough one. I'd probably be an air traffic controller, a ski instructor or a football player – so watch out Keith. But I have to say I love my job and that's down to a great support team behind me and all the positivity from the children. That keeps me going ... so ho, ho, ho and a very Happy Christmas to everyone!

IRISH ALL THE WAY

PAT HICKEY

The young woman gazed through the rain-splashed apartment window and looked for a break in the leaden Dublin sky. 'There is no chance of seeing the first star this Christmas Eve,' she thought. 'Back home in Slovakia, the snow would be knee deep and the children would be decorating the Christmas trees with apples, oranges and other important Christmas symbols. An extra place would be set at the table for a stranger. But now it's time to move on and build my new life in Ireland,' she mused, 'Forget about Slovakia and its traditions, forget about Mamma's death, it's just us two now.'

She looked down at the sleeping three-year-old boy. He turned in his sleep and his luxuriant red locks of hair sparkled in the candlelight. 'Yes, we are both fully Irish now.'

She laughed quietly, remembering her mother's reaction to his Christian name. Josef Fintan. 'I know where the Josef came from but who or what is this Fintan?'

'His name was on the side of the Irish plane that took me to Dublin,' she replied. 'And he is one of Ireland's most famous saints – what better name for him?'

Yes, it was all part of being Irish and not going back – her statement of freedom.

Her heart sank as she thought about Mamma and the suffering she went through with cancer. 'What was it all for, the chemo, the side effects? Was it worth it?'

Now she lived in a foreign city, her new home city, making a new life. Only herself and the boy. It's Ireland all the way now, being Irish in every way. 'He will play football for the team that the children downstairs shout about, the Dubs, or proudly wear the green shirt of Ireland, just like Signor Trapattoni.' Yes, Ireland all the way.

She set out the white tablecloth and the table placings and chairs for three – for the boy, herself and the stranger who might come in the night. She put the holy water and the honey pot beside the Christmas candle. Moving to the small galley kitchen, she passed the Christmas tree with its apples, oranges, wax eggs and wrapped sweets on the branches.

Supper would be fish and she had twelve small courses of bites ready to go with it. Most importantly, she had the communion wafers bought from the Slovak shop in

Smithfield. And the red wine. 'Not a bad spread at all,' she congratulated herself. 'My holy supper.'

Yes, there's no Christmas Eve like an Irish Christmas Eve!

NOTES ON CONTRIBUTORS

CIARA GERAGHTY is the author of *Saving Grace* and *Becoming Scarlett*. She is working on her third novel *Finding Mr. Flood*. She lives in Dublin with one husband and three children. She would like a dog – she would call him 'George' – but her one husband feels that their three children are enough to be getting on with … she lives in hope.

JUDI CURTIN was born in London, but her family moved to Cork when she was eight. She taught for many years in a primary school and loved it, but could not forget her childhood dream of becoming a writer. Judi's first novel hit the shelves in 2003 and her first novel for children was published in 2005. Judi lives in Limerick.

CATHY KELLY was born in Belfast, brought up in Dublin and started her working life as a journalist in an Irish national newspaper, as both a news and feature reporter. She worked as the paper's film critic for five years, as well as being the agony aunt for seven years. She is one of Ireland's best-loved novelists. In 2005, she was appointed as a UNICEF Ireland Ambassador and has visited Mozambique and Rwanda as part of her role. Global Parenting – caring for children orphaned or affected by HIV/AIDS – is the focus of her work with UNICEF.

NIALL QUINN is the chairman of Sunderland AFC. He has been involved in professional football since 1983 as a player, manager and pundit, as well as chairman. Capped ninety-one times for the Republic of Ireland, twenty-one international goals made Niall his country's all time record goal-scorer at the time of his retirement. Widely recognised for his charity work, he donated the £1m plus proceeds of his 2002 benefit match to hospitals in Sunderland and Ireland. Niall has continued to give his constant support to many worthwhile causes as he endeavours to use the power of football to become a force for positive change.

KATE GAYNOR is a graduate of University College Dublin with a BA degree in English and Sociology. Her books deal with a wide variety of issues, including introducing dyslexia, autism, Down's syndrome and hearing difficulties in a unique and child-centred way to readers. She currently works and lives in Dublin.

MAEVE BINCHY is an Irish novelist, newspaper columnist and speaker. She was educated at University College Dublin, she worked as a teacher then a journalist at *The Irish Times* and later went on to become a writer of novels and short stories. She lives in Dalkey, County Dublin, with her husband Gordon Snell, who is also a published author.

YVONNE CASSIDY was born in 1974 and grew up in Dalkey, County Dublin. She has written short stories, television scripts and is a regular reviewer for UK magazine *The Tablet*. Yvonne's first novel, *The Other Boy*, was published in May 2010, and she is currently working on her second, *What Might Have Been Me*.

Tom O'Neill had his book *Old Friends: The Lost Tales of Fionn Mac Cumhaill* published recently. He likes writing as it allows him to spend time interfering in the lives of strange and interesting characters, and it lets him make up lies that confuse and entertain people. His other interests include magic, science, farming and restoring ancient castles.

Jean Flitcroft lives in Dublin with her husband and three boys. She studied science in UCD and obtained her doctorate from Magdalen College, Oxford University. She became a script writer for medical and scientific films and later a travel writer. It was on these journeys around the world that she started writing books for children. Her first novel *The Cryptid Files: Loch Ness* was published in March 2010.

Joanna Binchy was born in Dublin and now lives in Charleville, County Cork with her husband and two children. She has written three children's novels: *The 13th of August Curse*, *The Green Diamond* and *The Black Toadstool*.

Neville Sexton lives with his partner Barbara Sinnott in Gorey, County Wexford. They have two children, Craig and Dean. Neville has written a book about their eldest son, Craig, who died on 2 November 2006, *The Boy Who Lives* (due out in Spring 2011). It was written in tribute to Craig's life, love and inspiration.

Dermot Bolger was born in Dublin in 1959, and is a well-known poet, playwright and novelist, having written nine novels and numerous plays.

PAULA LEYDEN was born in Kenya, grew up in Zambia and then moved to South Africa where she worked as a teacher and a human rights worker. In 2003 she moved to Ireland and now lives, farms and writes in Kilkenny with her partner, author Tom O'Neill, and their five children. Paula started writing fiction when she moved to Ireland and her first book for children will be published in March 2011.

TERRY PRONE has written for every national paper, is a columnist with the *Irish Examiner* and a regular commentator for the *Sunday Tribune*. She has also appeared on nearly every current affairs programme in the nation and is a regular on *Today with Pat Kenny*. She had written her first book by the age of twenty-five, which led to twenty-five others, several becoming best-sellers. She is a founder director of the Communications Clinic.

GER GALLAGHER was brought up in Foxrock, Dublin and was educated at St Brigids Girls National School and the Ursuline Convent, Cabinteely. When Ger was thirteen her family moved to the island of Bahrain in the Middle East where her father worked, but Ger returned to Ireland to complete her education. She is the author of such books as *A Life Left Untold*, *Broken Passions* and *Shadow Play*.

DAN BOYD is the author of the popular children's book, *A Dublin Christmas* published in 2006. Born and raised in the United States, Dan and his wife Clare live in Dublin with their three young children.

FIONA CASSIDY is from Galbally in County Tyrone. She lives with her partner Philip and together they have five children. She has written two novels, *Anyone for Seconds?* and, most recently, *Anyone for Me?* She is currently working on her third book and teaches creative writing classes and facilitates workshops. For more information about Fiona check out her website www.fionacassidy.net.

FIACHRA SHERIDAN is a schoolteacher and author whose debut novel *The Runners* earned him comparisons with Roddy Doyle. Fiachra grew up in Dublin's north inner city and he is the son of writer and director Peter Sheridan and nephew of film director Jim Sheridan.

DECLAN FRY is a primary school teacher who lives and works in Mullingar, County Westmeath. For the past twenty years he has been writing plays *as Gaeilge* for Scoildrámaíocht, the Irish schools drama competition, and has written many short stories for children, mainly in verse.

SHIRLEY BENTON BAILEY lives in Dublin with her husband and daughter. Educated at Mary Immaculate College of Education, Limerick and NUI Galway, she worked full-time in IT for ten years before leaving the industry in 2009 to pursue her dream of becoming a writer. Her first women's fiction book, *Looking for Leon*, will be published next year.

MARIAN O'NEILL is the author of three novels, *Miss Harrie Elliott* and *Daddy's*; her third novel, *Seeforge*, was published by Pillar Press, the publishing house she and her husband, Stephen Buck, founded in 2004. Marian currently lives in Thomastown, County Kilkenny.

EDDIE HOBBS has written three personal finance books and has presented multi-award-winning television series for the national broadcaster RTÉ, including *Show Me the Money* and the 2005 blockbuster *Rip Off Republic*. He edits Ireland's personal finance magazine *You & Your Money* and writes a weekly column for the *Irish Daily Star* newspaper.

JACINTA MCDEVITT has published three best-selling novels: *Sign's On* (2002), *Handle With Care* (2003) and *Excess Baggage* (2004). She also has one hugely successful non-fiction book published – *Write A Book In A Year, Writing Workshop & Workbook* (2006). Jacinta is well known for her writing workshops, which she has given for Fingal County Council, various libraries in the Dublin area, writing groups, transition year students and others. Jacinta was born in Raheny, but lives in Malahide, County Dublin.

ROISIN MEANEY has lived mostly in Limerick city since the age of eight and a very nice place it is too. Since 2001 she has written seven novels and two children's books. You can find out more on www.roisinmeaney.ie.

GERALDINE O'NEILL was born in Lanarkshire, Scotland and has lived with her family in Daingean, County Offaly, since 1991. Her books are mainly set in Ireland in the 1950s and 1960s and include the

Tara Flynn trilogy. She has worked as a teacher for many years in Scotland, England and Ireland, and is delighted to have one of her children's stories published with the Jack and Jill foundation. Her latest book, *Sarah Love*, has just been published and she is currently working on her ninth novel.

PATRICIA SCANLAN was born in Dublin, where she still lives. Her books have sold worldwide and been translated into many languages. She is series editor of *The Open Door* books, a prestigious literacy project she helped develop, which has become a critical and commercial success internationally. She has written four books for the series and is involved in promoting adult literacy.

JASON EDWARDS grew up in England and moved to Ireland several years ago. He has worked as a banker, a kitchen assistant, a tax clerk, a pea picker and a waiter, and also somehow managed to pick up a degree in mathematics along the way. None of these had any bearing on his decision to become a writer other than giving him enough free time to daydream the various stories that he writes down in his spare time. Jason lives in Wexford with his wife, daughter and cat.

KEITH ANDREWS was born in Dublin and plays in midfield for Blackburn Rovers Football Club as well as the Irish soccer squad.

PAT HICKEY is the President of the Olympic Council of Ireland, a member of the International Olympic Committee and president of the European Olympic Committees.